P9-CJN-460

"MYRON, a wryly amusing new novel which celebrates the return of Myra Breckenridge."
—*Book-of-the-Month Club News*

"Cleverness crowds the landscape of MYRON and it's as campy as Vincent Price and as surreal as that bunny-rabbit."
—Christopher Lehmann-Haupt
The New York Times

"Those who enjoyed Myra Breckenridge will enjoy her reincarnation and transformation as Myron."
—*Columbus Citizen-Journal*

"MYRON, the sequel to MYRA BRECKENRIDGE, is as perverse and strong in satiric implications as its predecessor. Its elaborate plot, though perfectly clear, is indescribable. Vidal's satire is beautifully conceived to cover not only movies and sex but a wealth of American institutions. MYRON is the unexpectedly perfect completion of MYRA BRECKENRIDGE. MYRON, howlingly funny, will be wildly read and unlike most bestsellers, enduring."
—*Library Journal*

"Literature's most famous transsexual is back as the star of Gore Vidal's latest camp fantasy. Give credit where credit is due . . . *Myron* is both funky and funny."

—*Chicago Sun-Times*

"Truly this is a tale for all tastes, satiric and philosophical, gay and mystical, gossipy and pornographical."

—*Philadelphia Inquirer*

"Gore Vidal's new one is ever-so-clever and campy."

—*Saturday Review/World*

"It's vintage nostalgia . . ."

—*Variety*

"Another kinky shaft into the motherlode of hard-Gore pornography."

—*Boston Globe*

"MYRON is predictably an outrage. But that's not all that's good about it. The novel is foul, silly, unpatriotic, offensive, clever and according to the standards of some communities, obscene."
—*The New Haven Register*

"Of course, Vidal is a master farceur—vulgar, autocratic, quaint . . . suave and exuberant, the master of a cool if mellifluous prose touched with a demotic tang."
—*The New York Review of Books*

"For MYRON, he (Vidal) tricks out his peeves and hostilities with the malicious energy that has made him the best—if not the most original—of our hard-core satirists. Myra/Myron is the perfect mate for Vidal's cold-blooded gifts."
—*Time Magazine*

"Vidal will delight fans anxious for a return to Myra Breckenridge's super kinky camptown . . . he wields a satiric needle sharp enough to keep his readers in stitches."
—*Newsweek*

By GORE VIDAL

FICTION

Williwaw
In a Yellow Wood
The City and the Pillar
The Season of Comfort
A Search for the King
Dark Green, Bright Red
The Judgment of Paris
Messiah
A Thirsty Evil (seven short stories)
Julian
Washington, D.C.
Myra Breckenridge
Two Sisters
Burr
Myron

PLAYS

Visit to a Small Planet and Other Television Plays
Visit to a Small Planet
The Best Man
On the March to the Sea
Romulus
Weekend
An Evening with Richard Nixon

ESSAYS

Rocking the Boat
Reflections Upon a Sinking Ship
Homage to Daniel Shays, Collected Essays 1952–1972

MYRON

by Gore Vidal

A Novel

BALLANTINE BOOKS • NEW YORK

Copyright © 1974 by Gore Vidal

All rights reserved.

Library of Congress Catalog Card Number: 74-9052

SBN 345-24625-X-175

This edition published by arrangement with
Random House, Inc.

First Printing: May, 1975

Printed in the United States of America

BALLANTINE BOOKS
A Division of Random House, Inc.
201 East 50th Street, New York, N.Y. 10022
Simultaneously published by
Ballantine Books, Ltd., Toronto, Canada

For George Armstrong

A recent decision of the Supreme Court leaves to each community the right to decide what is pornography. Speaking for the majority of the Court, Chief Justice Warren Burger admitted that although no link has yet been found between the consumption of pornography and anti-social behavior, any community may assume that such a connection exists if it wants to—in other words, an outraged community may burn a witch even though, properly speaking, witches do not exist.

The Court's decision has of course alarmed and confused the peddlers of smut, who claim, disingenuously, that guidelines are now lacking. They complain that the elders of Drake, North Dakota, may object to the word "damn" in a novel while the swingers of L.A. may want to read even worse words. Must the publisher, they ask, bring out two editions, one for permissive L.A. with the word "damn" and another for high-toned Drake with the word "darn"? Or settle the matter by publishing only for Drake?

This is a deep problem which I have solved. Wanting in every way to conform with the letter as well as the spirit of the Court's decision, I have carefully eliminated from this book those words that might cause distress to any one. Since books are nothing but words, a book is pornographic if it contains "bad" or "dirty" words. Eliminate those "bad" or "dirty" words and you have made the work "clean."

In this novel I have replaced the missing bad words with some very good words indeed: the names of the justices who concurred in the Court's majority decision. Burger, Rehnquist, Powell, Whizzer White and Blackmun fill, as it were, the breach; their names replace the "bad" or "dirty" words. I have also appropriated the names of Father Morton Hill S.J. and Mr. Edward Keating, two well-known warriors in the battle against smut. I believe that these substitutions are not only socially edifying and redemptive but tend to revitalize a language gone stale and inexact from too much burgering around with meaning.

MYRON

1

I don't know where I am but wherever it is that I am I have to get out of here pronto!

As the late sodomist and film critic Myra Breckinridge used to say, if you keep notes about where you are, you can always figure out sooner or later where it is in relation to other things. Naturally, I don't usually feature her advice or views on anything, as they are repellent to me as her successor and *true* self but I think that maybe in my present situation she had the right idea, as I am confused repeat confused not to mention upset by what just happened to yours truly Myron Breckinridge.

Now then—easy does it. One, to the best of my knowledge I am caught inside the movie *Siren of Babylon,* starring Maria Montez and Bruce Cabot, a picture made at Metro in 1948 and released in 1949 and one which I have seen, oh, maybe thirty times on the Late Late Show, where I was watching it again last night with this account book on my knees, trying to make sense of my wife and better half Mary-Ann's entries of income and outgo in our "San Fernando Chinese Catering to Your Home Service."

We had been watching the movie together downstairs in the rumpus room when around the sixth com-

3

mercial, the one for Turtle Oil Cosmetics, Mary-Ann said she was going up to bed, and I said, "O.K., honey. I'll be up just as soon as I've added up these old digits."—And she said, "You hurry up now," and tossed her head the way Marilyn Maxwell used to do in the film clips they used in the Empathy class at the Academy of Drama and Modeling where I met her six years ago when I was not myself but one of the teachers known as *Myra* Breckinridge, a woman whose career I prefer to forget and do forget except sometimes when I sit down with ball-point in hand to write a letter to the Van Nuys local paper on behalf of capital punishment or against smut and suddenly find that something very like Myra is trying to get out of the tip of my ball-point. I'd be a fool if I didn't know that she was lurking somewhere inside me, but since that hit-and-run accident just as I stepped out of the car in Santa Monica Canyon which knocked Myra and her famed knockers to bits, I have been *me,* my real self, a straight shooter, living with Mary-Ann the sort of American life that has made this country great, with our Chinese Catering Service and of course the silky terriers we breed. Like the President says, the American dream has been won for most of us who work hard and support our country and various community churches and organizations throughout this great land of ours in spite of the heavy burden of the people on welfare that we are forced to carry on our shoulders as a result of the crushing tax burden we have inherited from earlier, socialist-minded administrations.

You must forgive this digression but I am, as you can tell, trying to keep my sanity by deliberately reminding myself of the U.S.A. and the San Fernando Valley and my wife Mary-Ann and everything that is normal and American because at about one-oh-seven this morning I leaned over to the TV to turn down the volume and fell or was pushed—if so, by whom—who? —into *Siren of Babylon* at the point where the Priestess

4

of the Sun, Maria Montez, wearing a golden metal bra and with this tall golden crown on her head, appears at the top of a flight of stairs with these big plaster horses with wings on either side of her and these priests in white old-fashioned nightgowns, some holding spears, others holding and banging drums.

2

Myra Breckinridge lives! Like World War II hero General Douglas MacArthur, "I have returned." Yet colorful as corncob-pipe-sucking dugout Doug was, his panache was nothing compared to that of the second husband of his first wife Louise, the immortal Lionel Atwill, who stunningly outacted Errol Flynn in *Captain Blood* (1935.) It is a curious coincidence that when Errol Flynn made his tipsy way to the john on a certain sad day in 1959, he echoed Louise Atwill's husband when he declared to his bibulous chums (amongst them, legend has it, the nubile Beverly Aadland), "I shall return!" But Errol did not return. An hour later he was discovered on the bedroom floor, cold as a mackerel.

No mackerel Myra, cold or otherwise! For six years, since that terrible moment in front of my house when I was shattered by a mysterious car, I have bided my time, gathered my resources, prepared an agenda which, very simply, will restore me to my former glory and the world to its golden age: 1935–1945, when no irrelevant film was made in Hollywood, and our boys—properly nurtured on Andy Hardy and the values of Carverville as interpreted by Mickey Rooney, Lewis Stone, Fay Holden and given the world by Dream Merchant Louis B. Mayer

—were able to defeat the forces of Hitler, Mussolini and Tojo.

Since 1948 it has been downhill all the way. It is—again—no coincidence that the accident which put me out of commission in 1967 was directly responsible for the presidency of Richard M. Nixon, the current energy and monetary crises and the films of S. Peckinpah. I do not exaggerate: *All these disasters are the direct result of my removal from a scene which I was on the verge of transforming entirely.* Proof? Without me everything has gone haywire. Fortunately, I am back in the saddle again, ready to save the world at the eleventh—twelfth?—hour.

I will not dwell on my own private tragedy. Suffice it to say that being trapped inside a Chinese caterer in the San Fernando Valley, with, admittedly, a big restructured rehnquist between his legs but no powells, is not my idea of a picnic. But self-pity is not box office. Enough to say, I have come through!

Yes, it was I who *pushed* Myron Breckinridge into *Siren of Babylon.* After twenty years as a film critic, there is nothing I don't know about how to break into the movies.

3

I must've passed out or something from nervous exhaustion, because when I came to, sitting at this table in this hotel room where I am, I was numb in both legs from having sat sound asleep for what my watch says is one hour.

A funny thing. Someone has been writing something very funny in this account book. I can't read a word of what they wrote, as it is backwards-looking. I held it up to the mirror just now but I still couldn't read in. Anyway, so many crazy things are happening to me that this, at this point in time, is the least of my worries. Where was I? Even more to the point: Where am I? Well.

One minute I was fiddling with the volume knob of the TV and then there was this awful pushing and sucking sensation and suddenly there I was on my fanny about a yard away from Bruce Cabot, who is commander of the Babylonian royal guard as well as the rightful king of Babylon though he does not know yet that his rightful place was taken from him in childhood by Louis Calhern, who plays Nebuchadnezzar on whose dining-room wall God is going to write a pretty tough message in a later reel just before destroying Babylon.

At first I just couldn't believe it. I had gone from the middle of the night in our TV and rumpus room to outdoors where the sun was shining real hot and all around me those extras in Babylonian costumes and technicians were wandering about. In front of me was this tall staircase made of wood that was painted to look like marble. Just off to my left was Bruce Cabot, who was smoking a cigarette and picking his nose. I just sat there in the dust wondering if I was dreaming or not. Well, I am not dreaming I have now decided, having been here for several hours.

I must've sat there for maybe five minutes or so, with all these extras and other people acting as if I wasn't there. The movie that you see on the TV was sort of stopped from where I sat. That is, I wasn't really *in* it but just on the *edge* of it while it was still actually being made like twenty-five years ago. The scene I've seen so many times on TV was about to be made. A director or somebody shouted from somewhere behind me, "O.K., people, pipe down. We're going to start rolling."

Then somebody else said, "Cue Miss Montez," and then a makeup man came up to Bruce Cabot (born Jacques de Bujac in Mexico—how do I know that?) and said, "You've got a bit of shine, Mr. Cabot."

"Yeah, I'm sweating like a horse in this burgering blanket," said Bruce Cabot, as the makeup man powdered Mr. Cabot's face—all this just a few feet away from where I was sitting, out of my mind.

Sitting there on the ground in the hot sun, I decided that I was not in a dream but on the back lot of Metro-Goldwyn-Mayer, which I recognized from earlier visits when I was Myra Breckinridge. Just outside what they call the sight line of the movie, which is the picture that you see on the screen, were all these permanent and unpermanent sets: a railroad station next to this big water tank, and in front of some real woods off to one side there were maybe fifty different staircases set side by side—some straight, some spiral, going from

9

nowhere to nowhere like the one in front of me—lined with costume extras in their nightgowns, down which Maria Montez is about to come.

"O.K.!" a voice shouted from behind me. I turned to see where it came from, but saw that where the camera and the director and so forth ought to be there was nothing but this milky gray-blue square of nothing—sort of like the glass of your TV set when the light is on but there is no picture.

"We're starting to roll. Quiet on the set. Miss Montez, Mr. Cabot. Ready."

Then another voice—the director?—shouted, "It's magic time, children! Camera! Action!" And everybody got real quiet, even the technicians outside of the sight line.

The extras on the staircase began to bang their drums while these trumpeters at the bottom of the stairs blew this terrific blast. Bruce Cabot got rid of his cigarette and started to look very worried, which is what the scene calls for. I guess I know the picture by heart.

I got to my feet, still surprised that nobody had noticed me. "Civilians" like they call us who are not, thank God, in the movie industry are seldom welcome during the making of a picture, except of course on the special Universal City guided tour which Mary-Ann and I take at least three times a year when the in-laws are in town, and never get tired of.

Suddenly at the top of the stairs appeared Maria Montez. I'm afraid my heart just stopped. In spite of my predicament and my overall dislike of the movies, I was overwhelmed to be able to actually see this great star in the flesh.

For a moment Maria Montez just stood there at the top of the staircase, looking proud and disdainful, and everybody stared back at her with awe, including me. I can tell you it was a really funny feeling to be able to see the original of a scene I have seen so many times on the TV in actual three-dimensional real-life color as well as from a different angle, since I was able to look all around the set in every direction except where the director and the camera are.

Maria Montez is fabulously beautiful in real life, despite what looked like a coat of spar varnish on her face. She was the idol of my mother Gertrude the practical nurse who actually took me once years ago to see Maria Montez in the flesh when I was a kid and had been going through this sort of breakdown and for several weeks was out of my head, though I don't remember anything except Gertrude saying, "You were nuttier than a fruitcake." Anyway, Maria Montez was the first star I ever saw in the flesh and seeing her jolted me back to life, so Mother claimed, at the opening of Penney's in L.A.

Awful as the fix I am in is, I have to admit that it was a privilege a little while ago to see Maria Montez descend the staircase, her hips moving in this suggestive way as the priests banged those drums.

About halfway down the staircase Miss Montez stopped and said in this loud voice with a sort of Puerto Rican accent, "Hail, oh, commander of our far-flung armies!" I was so overcome I started to go over to where she was standing and ask—I don't know what. Maybe for the nearest exit.

"Out of the sight line, stupid!" a voice hissed in my ear.

I turned to see this fat small man with a big, bald pug-dog head and a damp-looking face like Peter Lorre with the same sort of damp-sounding voice that could make Chinese mushrooms grow even in your driest attic.

"Call me Maude," the small man Maude said, "and *get out of camera range*. Not that you'd show up in the movie as anything except a mike shadow, but the rules are the rules."

I was too stunned to say anything, much less understand a word he was saying, and so I let him steer me to the edge of the set where I could see the steel scaffolding behind the so-called marble staircase. Behind the set there were a half dozen extras and a dozen or so technicians all reading racing forms. They paid no attention to us because, Maude told me later, *they aren't able to see us.* This place is awful. But first things first.

Bruce Cabot pushed out his chest and walked to the foot of the staircase and said, "Hail, Priestess of the Sun. I come to high Babylon to make sacrifice to the oracle."

"Yea, you do well," said Maria Montez in her magical voice. It's funny, but I guess that over the years I have, without knowing it, learned all the dialogue by heart. Even so, it's scary hearing it like this from inside . . . inside *where?* We'll get to that.

Then Maude pulled this small worn-out-looking booklet from his pocket and began to flip through the pages as though he were bored to death. This booklet is titled "Orientation of New Arrivals to *Siren of Babylon.*" Maude confesses to a bad memory and always has to look at what's written down when somebody new arrives.

Maude started rattling instructions. But I couldn't really take them in.

"I guess this is a dream," I said.

"No, sweetie, it's not a dream. You're one of us now and you've made a *classic* entrance! Everybody who really matters comes in during this scene. It's fun and it's chic. We keep a twenty-four-hour watch and today it was my turn to greet the new arrivals and tell you that you must learn to stay out of the picture frame or what we call the 'sight line' when the camera is actually rolling. Then, let me see . . . Oh, yes, the farther back you are from the camera and the action, the nicer it is because . . . Hold on tight, sweetie! We're about to *FADE TO BLACK!*"

FADE TO BLACK is a movie term which means the scene you're looking at is going to fade out until it is black and then start over again fading into the light of the next scene. Well, this is O.K. when you're watching the movie but when you're caught *inside* the movie it is just horrible. I tell you I have never felt anything like that first *FADE TO BLACK*. I still can't get over it. Suddenly everything starts to go dark all around you like when you're about to faint. Then for what seems like forever you're surrounded by the blackest black you ever saw and you feel this awful weight pressing in on you from all sides like when you're deep under water and can't breathe.

Then just like when you come up to the surface for air, you suddenly *FADE TO LIGHT* and there you are in the next scene, which in this case was a section of the Temple of the Sun where there is this hole in the floor out of which comes steam from a block of dry ice that you don't see in the picture, naturally, but I was able to see from where I was standing. Beyond the hole is an altar on top of which stands Maria Montez in a different dress with a tiger-skin pattern and these huge earrings.

Bruce Cabot approaches her. "Oh, Priestess, I come to hear the oracle and learn the fate of our expedition to the land of ice and storm." Mr. Cabot was always a much underestimated star, as was Maria Montez, whose untimely death just three years after making *Siren of Babylon* in a hot paraffin bath at Elizabeth Arden's after taking too many reducing pills caused Myra to think seriously about the idea of becoming a Roman Catholic so that she could wear a mantilla and offer prayers for Maria's soul in St. Patrick's Cathedral, New York. Myra was like that. She would try to upstage even Miss Montez in death.

Why am I writing so much about Myra when my surgeon and mental-adviser Dr. Mengers and everyone is in agreement that I must simply block out that awful period of my life? I guess it's being here in this movie that has got me to thinking like they say at the think-tanks the unthinkable.

Shaken up as I was, I still wanted to watch the rest

of the scene, but Maude had my arm in a tight grip and before I knew it, we were outside the set, heading away from the production.

"At least you didn't get sick." Maude sounded very pleased. "The first *FADE TO BLACK* is quite an experience. Some of the toughest studs you ever saw throw up all over Bruce Cabot and sometimes they cry for days afterwards. As a matter of fact, *your* eyes look red." Maude gave me a suspicious look. I think he was wearing eyeliner and is a fag, an element I do not mind when they keep to themselves and do not prey on minors or solicit straight people like yours truly. Or hold these parades down Hollywood Boulevard and talk about Gay Lib.

I told Maude I was not about to cry. "You see, I've been watching first the Late Show and then the Late Late Show and that's why my eyes are red. Now if this isn't a dream, then where are we?"

"Well, let's put our thinking cap on, shall we? Isn't it pretty obvious that you've just joined our little colony inside *Siren of Babylon,* which is currently being filmed on the back lot of Metro the summer of 1948."

Maude took a quick peek at the booklet. Maude is something of a scatterbrain. "Oh, silly me," said Maude. "I can never remember all these facts and Mr. Williams fusses so if the newcomer is not thoroughly briefed." Maude's high voice became official-sounding. "Our little colony dates all the way back to 1950, when *Siren of Babylon* was first shown by special arrangement with Metro on TV because it bombed so badly at the box office. As of 1948—this year—Metro is over six million dollars in the red but Dore Schary has now taken over the studio and he will save the day or so the locals back here in 1948 think."

My head was going around. "Stop. Wait a minute. You mean that there are a lot of other people here who got caught in the picture like me?"

"Tons! What year is it back where you come from? 1972?"

"1973. But . . ."

"Hang on to my arm, sweetie! Here comes a *CUT TO!*"

Watching your average movie you hardly notice the *CUT TO* which is simply one scene taking the place of another real fast without a *DISSOLVE* which is a slow fade or a *FADE TO BLACK* which is just hell. Well, the *CUT TO* was like being flung across a room by a giant hand or swung about in one of those dodgem-cars at the fun-fair.

Suddenly we were dumped down outside the black walls of Babylon where the enemy army is standing. I can't get over the way you go from scene to scene in the picture just the way you do when you're watching it, only in this case *you're in it*. Maude takes all this for granted and pays no attention to the movie.

"I got here in 1961," said Maude. "Which makes me one of the old settlers. I don't mind telling you there was quite a stuffy group running things when I got here, but in the last few years we've been getting some really—what's that wonderful new phrase?—'groovy cats.'"

Just then a small fat old man of fifty or so with a full head of wiry gray hair and wearing a sort of white apron came running toward us. "Rehnquist-suckers!" he shouted at the soldiers in front of the painted canvas brick wall of Babylon. "Not one of you has the guts to stand up and fight a real man!" He started bobbing and weaving like a prizefighter who is punch drunk or in this case just plain drunk, which he turned out to be. The soldiers ignored him because they can't see him or any of us. That's one of the rules I will get to presently.

"I spoke too soon!" Maude moaned. "In every Eden there is a snake. That's ours. Whittaker Kaiser. He's a cook from Philly, and you know how cooks are!

All those hot stoves, all that frying, all those flambés! This one is a perfect menace."

Whittaker kept on dancing and shadowboxing around the dozen soldiers, his large cook's blackmun wobbling like a bale of live cats.

"He's only been here a few weeks and we all hope to God he starts to cool it soon. Sweetie, what's your exact date of arrival by the way?"

"April 16, 1973," I said. "No. It was after midnight, so it must be April 17." I confess that that drunk cook was making me nervous because cooks always carry knives somewhere on their persons.

"You'll get an identity disk when we get to the Strip."

"Bastards!" shouted Whittaker to nobody in particular. "Let me out of here!"

"I must say that keating-heel is driving us all straight up the wall with his flabby machismo. If it wasn't for this lady back at the Strip, who every now and then beats him up, we . . . Oh, God, here he comes!"

Whittaker came toward me, head down like a drunken heifer. "They're all fags in this picture! Like you! You're both fags!"

"Oh, shut up, Whittaker!" Maude sniffed. "And stay out of the sight line. One of these days you're going to be seen by the director of this picture and we'll all be in the soup."

"I can certainly outact and outfight and outburger Bruce Cabot." Whittaker's eyes are small, with this glazed look that all your cooks have. I know, since I am in Chinese Catering and must deal with cooks day in and day out. Admittedly this cook is still shaken up over having got caught in this old movie, but so am I and so are we all but that's no reason for him to carry on like some kind of loon.

"Of course you can, sweetie. You're the tops!" Maude gave me a wink. "But the rules are *stay out of the camera frame.*"

"Where," I asked, *"is* the camera?"

"There isn't one. That's the joke around here." Whittaker was dancing around me, making little boxing jabs and feints. But that stopped when we hit a *DISSOLVE TO,* which is almost as unpleasant as a *FADE TO BLACK* because during the worst part of it you're in two places at once: the scene you were just in outside the walls of Babylon and the next scene which happened to be the banquet hall of Nebuchadnezzar.

Luckily Maude had maneuvered us some distance away from the set, so that the *DISSOLVE TO* was not as painful as it is when you're at the edge of the action and are forced to go through the movie at the same rate it takes to unreel, which in the case of the TV version of *Siren of Babylon* is one hundred minutes of which twenty-one minutes are commercials and station breaks in which everybody freezes on the set and if you want to you can walk around on the set because everyone is frozen stiff and the camera isn't recording.

Important point: if you stand on the *camera* side of the action you have this entirely different sense of time, because you are really back in 1948 when the picture is being made and since it took eight weeks to make the picture I guess you could stay on the camera side the full eight weeks and see the whole thing being made. Anyway, for the record, that was where I first arrived—the camera side. Then Maude got me to the *other* side and I started to go through the picture as it plays until Maude, finally, got us out of the action. Apparently the farther away you get from the filming the more slowly you go through the picture, until about halfway across the back lot you are out of the movie altogether though you can still see it slowly, slowly unwinding back to front because you're now behind it. From the far end of the back lot the picture looks like a big drive-in movie screen hanging there in the sky.

"How do you know there's a camera?" I said,

thinking of what Whittaker had just said. "I can't see one."

"Because . . . What's your name sweetie?"

"Myron. I'm in Chinese Catering in the San Fernando Valley."

"You're not a cook, are you?" Maude looked alarmed until I explained about my business and Mary-Ann and the dogs. God, how I missed them! While I was talking, Whittaker kept eyeing me. Finally he said, "My rehnquist is bigger than your rehnquist."

"Whittaker!" Maude shrieked with delight.

"I doubt that," I said coolly, knowing what a remarkable thing Dr. (formerly Nurse) Mengers was able to make for me after I was run over by that car and lost forever, I am happy to say, Myra's silicone father hills and so was able after the auto accident to be restored to my original manhood, except of course that I had had my male organs removed some years ago in Denmark when I was Myra and so it took all of Dr. Mengers' genius to roll a sizable cylinder of skin and flesh from the inside of my left thigh. "You dressed on the left originally, did you not, Mr. Breckinridge? Then you will do so again, thanks to Miracle Mengers!"

This large artificial rehnquist was then attached to what had been my—or rather Myra's—whizzer white, and all, or nearly all, your usual blood vessels and odds and ends were hooked up by one of the finest surgeons it has been my good luck to meet in the greater L.A. area. The fact that I had a certain amount of hair on the inside of my thigh meant that at first my rehnquist was sort of furry and funny-looking. But then electrolysis came to the rescue and now I am clean as a whistle.

The result is extremely decorative and I am a sensation in the shower room at the Y, even though, to tell the truth, I do not have much feeling in this new part except for a bit on the underside where sensitive skin from my wrist was grafted. But as Mary-Ann says, love is all in our heads anyway, and it is true that we have a perfect marriage and one day when our joint workload lessens somewhat I will have Dr. Mengers make me a set of powells.

"Of course, they will only be for show, Mr. Breckinridge," said Dr. Mengers. "They won't work. But you'll find the overall effect is much dresser and good for morale. I guarantee that you will never regret the money you invest in a Miracle Mengers' Scrotum, the perfect gift for the man who has nothing!" Dr. Mengers is very witty for a surgeon.

"Ah'm gonna knock the kee-yeat-ing out of yee-ooh," said Whittaker, suddenly talking like some sort of hillbilly. He then pulled a bottle from his pocket and took a drink of whiskey.

"You're drunk," said Maude.

"There's a lot to be said for being drunk."

"Must you say it all, sweety?"

Whittaker was looking very mean, even for a cook. This place has clearly made him crazy. After three hours here I can see why.

For absolutely no reason Whittaker lowered his head and charged at *me*. I stepped to one side and he fell over a bush just as we *CUT TO* the wharf at Tyre where Bruce Cabot is about to set sail for Ultima Thule.

"We *know* there's a camera," said Maude, returning to the subject at hand, "because we can *hear* the director's voice from time to time."

"It's a trick!" Whittaker was on his feet again; he had dropped the hillbilly accent. "They just *pretend* there is a director."

"There *has* to be a director, sweety, because we've all seen the movie and we've all read the credits over and over again and we know that this picture was directed by Benjamin R. Laskie. So out there, somewhere"—Maude gestured at the blue-gray horizon—"Benjamin R. Laskie in June and July of 1948 is shooting *Siren of Babylon* on the back lot at Metro."

"You *think* he's out there. Well, I happen to know that he's not out there, rehnquistsucker."

Maude drew himself up. "Whittaker, I am reporting you for trying to break frame. Come, Myron. We've got to get you registered."

We left Whittaker trying to get on board the false ship where Bruce Cabot was standing looking out to the sea which was painted on a large piece of canvas and hung from a derrick. Every time Whittaker would try to crawl up onto the boat, a heavy-set man would pull him off. No one else paid any attention to him.

"The big fellow is Luke. He's on duty during this scene."

"Why can't the actors see Whittaker?"

"Because nobody can see us who's actually in the movie. In fact, we're invisible to everybody in this part of the back lot, although Mr. Williams . . ."

"Who?"

"*Our* director. He was the first arrival. Mr. Williams insists that even so we must be very, very careful not to break frame—you know, get in range of the camera—because sometimes we're apt to show up as shadows or smudges, especially in the background shots. I must say, thinking about it makes my head ache. So I don't. I suggest you do the same. Just 'ride the film' like we say on the Strip."

Maude and I were now at the halfway point between the movie and the end of the back lot. "Pretty, isn't it?"

Maude turned to show me for the first time the movie unreeling in the sky. It is quite a sight. Half the sky at this point is filled with the movie, while there is this thin bright line all about whatever is being photographed at the moment and shown on your TV. Sometimes the line just makes a square around Maria Montez's face in Technicolor. Then the square will show you the hills of Mesopotamia in the summertime. It is really scary, that bright line forever forming these squares against the funny-looking blue-gray sky which hides where the camera is, where all the people are who are sitting at home tuned in to the Late Late Show courtesy of Dad-Freakness Used Cars, not knowing that they are watching some real people like Maude and Whittaker and me, smudges and shadows though we may look to you, as we try to get out of camera range, try to get out of this movie. Because that is the name of the game around here as I see it. Out!

4

So that blackmun Myron thought that he had destroyed me once and for all! Sooner destroy all memory of Helen Gahagan in the title role of *She* as obliterate from the face of the world—*this* world of holy celluloid—its one and only begetter, the archcreatrix herself who rises now as inexorable as Baron Frankenstein's creation when it emerged from beneath the fallen timber of Universal's Transylvanian castle, as minatory as the Karlovian hand of the mummy when it first twitched beneath that dusty millennial unguent-soaked wrapping, as poignant as Bela Lugosi when he drew from his heart the wooden stake, as cathartic as Lon Chaney, Jr., when he gouged from his furry chest the silver bullet!

Now let the enfolding night ring once again with the cries of the vampire bat, with the ululations of the were-wolf, with the monster's moan and hiss as he takes the flower from the little girl beside the twilit tarn! Because Myra is back in the saddle—without a wardrobe, I fear, and with insufficient control over the mutilated body I am forced to share with Myron Breckinridge. Happily, I have arranged for his demise in a matter of hours . . .

5

What's wrong with me? It's happened again. I passed out again and there is more writing I can't read in this account book. I guess I'm going crazy, but who wouldn't go crazy after the last few hours, I ask you?

Anyway, whoever is writing in this book better watch out, as I am in a mean and desperate mood. So where was I before the blackout? Out? Yes, *out*. Out is the name of the game.

Maude enjoyed being my guide through the back lot, putting away the booklet and chattering about all the interesting people caught like me inside the movie. Maude also showed me the different permanent sets. Some of them I dimly remembered from those awful years when I was Myra.

Just past a Swiss Alpine village street was the fence and gate to the back lot of Metro which is now (1973) about to be a housing development but now (1948) is still pretty fascinating because Hollywood is at its peak.

What Myra would have given to see the back lot the way I am seeing it! And how she would have cut her wrists if she could see what has happened to Hollywood in the five years it's been since *"She* left us," as Mary-Ann sometimes says, with a shudder, during which period of time the Kerkorian-Aubrey management has all but stripped MGM to the bone in order to build a colossal-type hotel in Vegas.

The guard at the gate was reading the *Hollywood Reporter* and paid no attention to us as we passed through. "He's used to us by now," said Maude.

"I thought nobody can see us."

"The dividing line is halfway into the lot. From the gate to the middle of the lot, they can see us. After that, they can't. If they did, we'd all be in pictures, wouldn't we? And of course we weren't."

At the time Maude might as well have been talking Latin for all the sense he was making to me at that moment.

Beyond the studio gate is the Strip—Thalberg Boulevard—which extends to the left and right in a straight line as far as the eye can see, which isn't too far because after what looks to be maybe a quarter mile in either direction of the studio gate there is a glassy mirage effect like on a hot day when you see lakes and puddles in the highway that aren't there from the sun. That's the end of the road for us "out-of-towners"—as we are known to the 1948 people, who are known to us as the "locals."

Across from the gate is the Irving Thalberg Hotel, a pink-stucco four-story Spanished-styled building with oleanders in the front yard and a red neon sign in which the word "Irving" does not light up. On either side of the hotel there is nothing but vacant lots filled with tin cans, remains of cars and a large billboard advertising *The Three Musketeers,* a Pandro S. Berman production—I seem to recall Berman was a favorite of Myra—starring Gene Kelly with Van Heflin, Gig Young and Robert Coote.

"That's home for most of us." Maude indicated the hotel. Cars sped past. Funny-looking old cars. Just past the vacant lot where the billboard is, is a Texaco gas station and just past that are two bungalows with neat gardens in front, with morning glories growing on trellises and hollyhocks by the door, the kind of garden Mary-Ann likes so much and has made for us in the Valley as a setting, she likes to say in a joking way, for her plastic Seven Dwarfs from Disneyland.

"Some of our group live back there, on the lot. Others board at those houses down the road or at the Mannix Motel. The Mannix is low-life, sweetie, but fun!" Maude's small paw indicated some tacky wooden cabins in the opposite direction from the Texaco station. Each cabin has a spindly wooden porch in front. On the crabgrass lawn in front of the main building of the Mannix Motel and Café a faded sign says *Vacancy*.

" 'There's always room at the Mannix' is an old saying around here. But what's really maddening is the movie house down there. See?" Beyond the motel cabins is the wall of a medium-size picture palace entirely covered by a huge sign advertising Henry Hathaway's *Call Northside 777*.

"Well, by some strange coincidence none of us has ever seen *Call Northside 777* and we can't see it now because the entrance to the theater is just past the end of the road—*our* end, that is—and there's no way we can get in from this side without blasting a hole in the theater, which of course Mr. Williams won't allow, since the first rule around here is never interfere with the locals. But I'm sure I told you that, didn't I?" Maude looked uneasy; a very forgetful-type queen.

All in all, my mind was absolutely blown by Maude's revelations. Up to a point I can see how you might *think* yourself inside a movie. People wander around doing that all the time at Buck Loner's Academy of Drama and Modeling where Myra used to teach Empathy, but it is totally demoralizing to find that you have thought yourself or been thought by somebody else into a place where there is a road which ends, just *ends* completely as far as you and the other out-of-towners are concerned even though this very same road keeps right on going for all the cars that whiz by and for any of the 1948 people who want to stop, say, and see *Call Northside 777*.

"Maude, I'm going to be sick." For a moment I thought that the trip through the movie had really done me in, particularly the knocking about you get during the *CREDITS* when all those names keep jerking past you and the MGM lion comes on, roaring and scaring the keating out of you because you can smell him, thirty times life-size.

"Sweetie, don't! You've made it this far. We're almost home." The nauseous feeling, thank God, passed. So I just belched and had a feeling that I had had this conversation before: what Myra used to call in French *déjà vu* because there is no English way of saying what it's like to be talking to a fat bald hairdresser called Nemo Trojan who wants to be known as Maude because he took over Chez Maude, a hairdressing establishment in White Plains from which, on the night of January 2, 1961, he fell into *Siren of Babylon*—and have the sense while talking to Maude on the edge of Thalberg Boulevard that I had had this exact conversation before.

Normally I would think that I was dreaming except that in your usual dream you can't read anything at all no matter how hard you try and I can read with no trouble "Thalberg Hotel," *Call Northside 777*, "Mannix Motel and Café," *The Three Musketeers*, not to mention the license plates on the passing cars which all date from 1948, the plates, that is. Some of the cars themselves ought to be in museums.

"Who," I asked Maude as we crossed the highway, "is this Mr. Williams you keep referring to?"

"I told you, sweetie. *Our* director. The first arrival." Maude was staring at the sky above the motel just as the sun suddenly went behind some dark stormy clouds. Maude shuddered. "I hate this time of day. Come on in and we'll get you registered."

It's funny, but it wasn't until I stepped into the

lobby of the hotel that I realized for the first time that I am really and truly stuck in the year 1948, a year I have already lived through once as a ten-year-old and now have come back to, through no fault or wish of my own, as a thirty-five-year-old caterer who should be living in the Valley a quarter of a century later, happy as can be with a great wife, only he's not because I have got somehow caught in a year which I didn't like all that much the first time around because I was ill most of the time.

I don't know why but the musty, dusty cleaning-wax smell of the lobby of the Thalberg reminded me suddenly of the way houses used to smell when I was a kid. The calendar back of the reception desk which said June 14, 1948, was pretty depressing as was the red plastic jukebox in one corner where the latest oldies are constantly played very low as the guests do not like loud music.

On a big table beside the door to the dining room there are magazines like *Collier's* and *Saturday Evening Post* and local newspapers and not one is dated later than June 14, 1948! I know. I checked. You can never rule out conspiracy in this day and age of revelation about the surveillance of—and even by—Federal officials, which is why, even now, I still don't rule out the fact that I have been drugged and that this is all a put-up job.

Back of the reception desk is the manager's office, where the radio was playing. A newscaster was telling all about how there is a new president of Czechoslovakia as well as trouble in Korea. I guess the Korean War over there hasn't begun yet. I wish I could remember more current events than I do but I don't have much of a memory for such things because Myra was always going to the movies in those years. In fact, from about the time I was, oh, twenty years old until I was thirty and got run over on Sunset Boulevard I was not myself but Myra Breckinridge. Mary-Ann who knew both of us says she can't really believe that Myra ever existed. Neither can I, thank God. That part of myself is gone with the wind like they say, starring Clark Gable, Vivien Leigh, Leslie Howard. Funny, there I go again, remembering movies.

"Mr. Myron Breckinridge," said Maude to the tall man behind the desk. "He's one of our party."

The tall man shook his head and frowned even though he never stopped smiling the whole time. He was actually born in California, I later learned. "I never seen *anything* like the business this time of year! Never! Not that I'm complaining! Just sign here please, sir."

I signed.

"I guess he'll be staying until . . ."

"Until July 31 when the picture stops shooting." Maude sounded rehearsed.

"Then what happens?" I asked.

"Why, we start all over again. You see, there are eight weeks of shooting beginning June 1 and ending July 31, 1948."

"Does *he* start all over again?" I lowered my voice, as I referred to the manager whose back was to us as he looked for my room key.

"Sweetie, say anything you like in front of him about our situation because whenever any of us talks about all *that,* we might as well be talking gibberish as far as the locals go."

As if to prove Maude's point, the manager turned around and showed us a lot more of his upper plate and an even deeper scowl as he said, "There you go again! It's been going on for two weeks now, all you out-of-towners coming here and talking this funny language. Well, just so long as it's not Russian, I say!" He laughed like he had made this joke before.

"I'll be in the bar, sweetie."

Maude vanished into the back part of the hotel while Mr. Van Upp, which is the manager's name, took me to the second floor and gave me a room looking onto the back yard. Just below my window was a kidney-shaped swimming pool, a bit scummy-looking but even so a number of good-looking girls in one-piece Jantzen bathing suits which show the shape but not the skin were lying around the pool, taking sunbaths though the sun was now gone behind the dark stormy ugly sky and it must, I thought, be about seven in the P.M.

"Won't they get wet?"

"That's what the pool's for, Mr. Breckinridge."

"No, I mean it's going to rain from the look of that storm."

Mr. Van Upp nodded like he had a secret. "Looks like rain to you, don't it?"

"Well, yes."

"You all say that. It's my guess—now, mind you, I don't want to pry—that you are all some kind of Masons with secret passwords, and so on. I was going to be a Mason once but my mother was a lapsed Catholic and you know what they're like. Mr. Williams is picking up your bill." Then he was gone.

I am suddenly absolutely miserable, sitting now in the middle of this small hotel room that smells of Dutch Cleanser and knowing it is the summer of 1948 when just a few miles away, over the hills, is my own house and wife—except the house isn't built yet and Mary-Ann isn't born yet and I am back in New Jersey aged ten except I'm not really. I'm really in the Thalberg Hotel.

I don't know what I'm going to do without my water pick for thorough dental hygiene. Must buy dental floss if it has been invented in this frame of time.

The phone just rang.

"This is Mr. Williams." The voice on the telephone was very high class and English like Claude Rains. "I trust you are comfortably lodged."

"Well, yes, sir, I am, but I have a wife and a business and just how long am I going to be in this place?"

"Until the last day of shooting. That will be in about six weeks."

"Six weeks! But Mary-Ann, she's my wife, she'll . . ."

"We must accept our situation, Mr. Breckinridge. We are inside *Siren of Babylon*. That is the principal fact of all our lives. The link, as it were, between us."

"But I want to get out."

"You will find your identification disk and orientation booklet at the desk. A small allowance will be paid you each Saturday by Mr. 'Rooster' Van Upp. Each Thursday you will stand guard at the Great Staircase—where you met Mr. Nemo Trojan formerly of Chez Maude—to greet anyone who may be joining us. You will bring him here as you were brought here. We shall be in communication, Mr. Breckinridge."

"But, Mr. Williams, I'd like to sit down and chew the rag with you about all this man to man."

"An appointment can be made at the desk. Write your name in Mr. Van Upp's book. And now good . . ."

"But . . . but. . . ." I am desperate for any information I can get, not to mention any human contact. "When did *you* get here?"

"In 1950, Mr. Breckinridge. *Siren of Babylon* was one of the first new pictures to be sold to television. I watched it, as a novelty. Good evening." Click.

Possible ways of getting out of here.

One: why not thumb a ride from one of the cars? Or if they won't stop for fear of muggers, go to the service station and pay somebody to drive me in to Hollywood. Of course, it would still be 1948 . . . or would it? Must find out. If it's still 1948 I could at least find my mother Gertrude the practical nurse and get to see myself at the age of ten years old and we could work something out.

Two: go back into the picture and try to get out the other side where the camera has got to be. Since that is the way I came in, that will probably be the best way to get out.

Three: . . .

I was interrupted and now I've forgotten what three was and it was important, I remember thinking, when I first thought of it.

The door to my room opened and this strange-looking girl with hair piled high on her head in front but hanging down her back in the back with a short dress and square shoulders and no stockings but wearing wedgies came into the room without any invitation and said, "I'm Iris. You're new. I saw you register. Let's have a roll in the hay."

The voice was throaty like Kay Francis but without the lisp and she was wall-eyed like Norma Shearer . . . I don't know why but something about this place is making me start to think about movies like Myra used to do. *I have to cool it.* I have got to be careful because all that is behind me. Myra is dead. And Myron lives . . . only I am living twenty-five crazy years ago!

"*Why* do you want to have a roll in the hay?" I played for time. She got down on the bed beside me. I saw that her thin lips were smeared with orange Tangee like Gertrude my mother the practical nurse. For an awful moment I thought maybe this *was* Gertrude my mother at age thirty, but of course in 1948 Gertrude was in Red Bank, New Jersey, with yours truly.

"I love all of you. I *want* all of you. Because you're different. You know something we don't." She took off her blouse. She was wearing a very elaborate bra just like Gertrude's. "Unhook me," she commanded. I unhooked.

The left father hill was only half the size of the right—and I was reminded suddenly of the proud perfectly matched pair of father hills shaped for me—for Myra—by the best surgeons in Europe, who

31

pumped golden silicone into me in order to create those twin glories that were destined so rudely to be deflated and drained as a result of that mysterious hit-and-run accident. Thank God, of course.

Iris started grabbing at me but I was firm and fought her off. Unlike your average Oedipus, I could never make love to anyone who looked like Gertrude. Besides, I did not exactly go for those ill-matched father hills with, I swear, one pink aureoled nipple and one brown!

Most important of all, I am true to Mary-Ann. Partly because Mary-Ann is the only girl in the world for me and partly because I have never looked forward to having to explain to some strange woman, no matter how sexy, how I never got around to ordering new powells because I have been too busy these last five years. Besides, Mary-Ann has been so happy with the unusually large rehnquist Dr. Mengers rolled for me from the skin from inside my left thigh that she has never really insisted on my investing in a set of Miracle Mengers powells.

"I don't appeal to you." Iris pouted when I pushed away her hand after first letting her get a good feel of Dr. Menger's handiwork. "You're a pansy, I'll bet."

"No, Iris. I am a married man, that's all. A happily married man. Your father hills don't match," I heard myself say without meaning to.

"Only a pansy would've noticed!" Iris was turning ugly, not to mention red in the face, as she struggled back into her old-fashioned bra.

"What year you from?"

"1973."

"Nineteen Lady Me! Hey, that's close. At least I got the nineteen. You realize I *almost* dug you, solid sender? Rooster says that's the question to ask."

"You couldn't hear what I said?"

"You think I'm deaf? Of course I heard you. But

like all you out-of-towners you make no sense. Can I blow you?"

"No, Iris. Thanks. But no thanks." Old films are beginning to fill up in my head as do things which were once a part of Myra's mind. I am very definitely getting uneasy.

"I blew Mr. Louis B. Mayer." Iris gestured toward the studio across the road. "When I was under contract a few years back. It was in his office during the lunch break. He had a hot pastrami sandwich at his desk while I was underneath. He spilled some mustard in my hair and said, 'Mustard-yellow! That's the best color for you, Rose.' He kept calling me Rose. I only saw him the once. Since then I model. Rooster is an old pal. He was under contract, too, but he saved his money. He was in *Thirty Seconds Over Tokyo*. Now he does real well with this hotel. At least this summer. He says he's never seen anything like all you out-of-towners, acting so strange. You know, the sheriff came by once to investigate because the people at the gas station are from Oklahoma and think your group are Communists and so they told the sheriff, who had a long talk with Mr. Williams and never came back."

"Have you met Mr. Williams?"

"Not really. He was the first to check in. I remember it was the first day of shooting of that new flick they're making now with Maria Montez and Bruce Cabot. I'd like to blow Bruce. I like him in pictures. He was really swell in *Sundown*. Did you see *Sundown*? Really nifty. You're certainly well-hung, Myron, I could feel."

"Thanks, Iris. But I just can't."

"Well, if you change your mind . . . I always like to strike while the iron is hot because when you people first get here there's something real different about you. I don't know what it is but it really sends me. Then after you're here a few days you get more or less like everybody else."

Food for thought: Rooster Van Upp knows more

than he lets on. Mr. Williams, too. As the first arrival, Mr. Williams must know what this is all about.

One more point: on the last day of shooting we go right back where we started from. But where is that? Home, I hope.

6

Myron's will is more powerful than I suspected. He must be broken. Soon. Because, frankly, I cannot take much more of this seesawing back and forth, this coming and going—particularly the going—when I have work to do!

A few minutes after the ill-groomed Iris left the room, I was able to replace Myron at the controls. But there was a struggle. In his cretinous way, he, too, shares the Breckinridge genius. But in the end of course he will be no match for me—nothing human is (or *non*-human for that matter, as I shall presently demonstrate).

Just now I went to the window. Took a dozen deep breaths of 1948 non-polluted ozone and started to tingle from top to toe; became giddy; almost drunk with joy.

Beneath my window, shadowy figures cavort beside the pool. As the boxer-trunked boys and Jantzened girls sunbathe in the dark, they look exactly like some of those extras I have so often glimpsed in the background of Esther Williams films—are they the very same boys and girls? It is perfectly possible. After all, we are next door to MGM and off-duty extras must cavort somewhere.

Despite the darkness, I was able to detect, here and there, an ominously bulging *pullulating* set of trunks. In-

35

voluntarily, I shuddered. The enemy has been sighted. *Operation Myra* now goes into phase one.

My moment of euphoria passed when, foolishly, I removed my—Myron's—clothes to get a good look at the work he has done to what was once, very simply, the body of the most beautiful woman the world has known since that tragic day when Vera Hruba Ralston hung up her ice skates at public request. *Hair* grows down my—no, not my: *his* ugly chest.

Worst of all, between my still gorgeous legs, within that sacred precinct where the finest of Scandinavia's surgeons once fashioned a delicate whizzer white as cunningly contrived as the ear of a snail, that son of a bitch Myron has not only removed the delicate honeypot of every real American boy's dreams but replaced it with A Thing! A ghastly long thick tubular object which must look to the casual onlooker—if such there be in my case! —as if it were some sort of vegetable on the order of *The Thing* (1952), a curiously religious film written by clever funster Charles Lederer, the nephew of Marion Davies; and starring James Arness, my *assiette de thé* if there ever was one, all six feet six of him, now lost to television.

This rehnquist has got to go! For one thing the overall effect is ghastly, since Myron was obviously too cheap to buy a pair of powells.

My once and future exquisite body has been hideously hacked and butchered by one Dr. Mengers, formerly Nurse Mengers, whom I always suspected of treachery even in the heyest of my days. The once and future glorious father hills have been deflated. Livid scars beneath each dull masculine nipple bear mute witness to those astonishing twins which for too brief a time made glorious the Hollywood of the late sixties.

I sit at this table (fully clothed—I cannot bear the sight of me—him!), and begin now to weave my web, to create my universe. And the first strand of this astonishing creation that I have in mind will be a proper wardrobe

—not to mention wig, eyelashes, silver detachable fingernails, etc.

Then once and for all, Myron must be suppressed. I
had thought that I could obliterate him simply through
the exertion of my will over his. But nut-wise he is harder
to crack than I thought. So I must now resort to my old
stand-by that never fails, the hormone cocktail. But has it
been invented yet? If not, I think I recall enough of the
formula to whip up a batch that will get this hair off
my chest and Myron out of my skull.

Removing the pseudo-rehnquist will be more of a problem, but I am sure that there are a dozen friendly surgeons in the area who will do the necessary snip-snip under hygenic working conditions. The rebuilding of my
glorious father hills, of my delectable whizzer white will
take more time, but have I not time enough to spare, since
this world is mine and all things in it?

To work! First, I shall save MGM at the most crucial
moment in the history of the motion picture industry
when, thanks to television, the studio system is about to
go down the drain, taking with it Andy Hardy, Maisie,
Pandro S. Berman, Esther Williams—everything, in fact,
that made America great, that made it possible for boys
to beat the keating out of Hitler, Mussolini and Tojo.

I shall personally take charge of all MGM production
during the coming crucial weeks, supporting the belea-
guered Dream Merchant Louis B. Mayer against the in-
terloper Dore Schary, whose sponsorship of *The Boy with
the Green Hair* (1948) marked the beginning of the end
of the golden age of the movies. By August 1 Schary will
be out on his blackmun and L. B., guided by me, will restore Metro's product to what it was before the release
of *The Boy with the Green Hair* and the advent of television's Milton Berle and Snookie Lanson.

It is important that I save not only Hollywood—the
source of the best of our race's dreams since those brut-
ish paintings on the cavern walls at Lascaux—but the
United States. For in a nation inspired by the values of
Andy Hardy's father, good Judge Hardy as played by

Lewis Stone—still alive and kicking as I sit in this dingy hotel room (I am home! home!)—the current age of darkness through which we are passing (1973) would never have taken place, for the simple reason that Richard M. Nixon could never have been elected President, while the films of S. Peckinpah would not have obtained financing from a major studio even with the return of block-booking, and block-booking is high on my agenda because the studios must own their own theaters again; so to hell with the Sherman Anti-Trust Act!

Once I have restored Hollywood to its ancient glory (and myself to what I was!), I shall very simply restructure the human race. This will entail the reduction of world population through a complete change in man's sexual image.

7

I knew it was you all along, you bitch Myra! I was just leading you on pretending I couldn't read that dumb disguised writing of yours which has to be read in a mirror but *upside* down, which is the way you see everything in your perverted way.

Well, you are not about to take over yours truly Myron Breckinridge, any more than you are going to take over MGM, which is a big laugh. Who over there will listen to you, you drag queen freak? Yes, that's what you are, and as for hormone cocktails, two can play at that party. By the time I finish taking *male* hormones I'm going to be covered with hair like a tarantula, with a voice way down in my powells when I buy them which will be soon, you can bet your sweet blackmun. Then *you* are going to be finished once and for all. Kaput. So put that in your whizzer white and suck it.

Meanwhile, I am getting out of here pronto because I am, like they say at the touch-and-feel sessions Mary-Ann and I used to attend in Encino, *highly motivated*. Get that, Myra? I have the best wife in the world and eight terriers and my catering and no crazy-type mad woman is going to keep me away from them. Warning. I am eating oysters tonight. That will put lead in my rehnquist like they say, and if I can find any prairie oysters I'll eat them and vitamin E, too, if it's been thought up yet. You've had it, Myra.

After writing this message to Myra, I went downstairs to the bar which is cozy with two glass doors that open out onto the patio where the pool is and where, even though it is dark, there are still people splashing around. Of course, it's a fairly hot evening, I thought in my innocence, and looked at my watch which said it was only five o'clock. I thought, having found out that it was Myra who got me into this picture and is now trying to take over, that I had learned the worst. Well, I hadn't. I was in for some pretty awful surprises, as I will recount.

In the bar there were half a dozen local people sitting at these round tables drinking beer and listening to Perry Como on the red and green plastic juke-box. It's funny, but you get so you can tell right away who is local and who is an out-of-towner. The locals if they are girls look like Iris with funny hair styles and short dresses with these squared-off shoulders. So far I have only seen one with a long dress on and she made everyone go buzz-buzz and talk about The New Look, whatever that is. The local men have short hair and wear wild-looking Hawaiian-style sports shirts with wide baggy trousers which totally disguise their baskets.

Maude was sitting with a lady in black who greeted me with "August 11, 1969." Good form in our group is to say on first meeting your day of arrival and the place you left from: "Plandome, New York." And your name: "Miranda Bowles. Mrs. Connally Yarborough Bowles."

I said my piece.

"Sit down, sweetie," said Maude. "Look what I've done with Miranda's hair with only this *ancient* equipment!"

"Maude has a gift," said Mrs. C. Y. Bowles, whose flame-colored hair had been teased into a beehive, suitable for 1961, the year that Maude left the real world.

"Bartender. A daiquiri for me with plenty of ice, and now—get this, sweetie—a full jigger of rum *on the side.*" Maude turned to me. "Have one, too." So I had one and so did Mrs. C. Y. Bowles. Maude I'm afraid was a little tipsy. "You know I'm a Paganini of hair!" Maude yelled after the second swallow of what must've been his third daiquiri.

"There's nothing I can't do with hair, no matter how dry or how thin or how frazzled at the ends. Doris Duke used to say 'Maude, you are supreme.' I also do the Duchess of Windsor when she's at the Waldorf."

"I thought your business was in White Plains."

"I'm *sent* for, sweetie. A talent like mine only comes once in a generation. Everybody wants Maude to *bend* their hair. Mr. Kenneth hates me but I don't give a hoot!" hooted Maude.

"It is odd, Mr. Breckinridge," said Mrs. C. Y. Bowles, "but I actually went to Maude some years ago at the recommendation of a dear mutual friend. Now deceased. From Plandome. Little did I dream that one day we would meet *here.* I am a widow," she added for no particular reason except she likes to keep adding these bits of information.

"Miranda's husband was a judge in New York."

"With the Appellate Court. Connally died July 4. I have a lime tree in the garden. The only one in Plandome. It must be taken in during the winter."

"Wowee!" Two adolescent boys, one tall and skinny and one short and skinny with hair plastered down from water and wearing boxer-type swimsuits, came running in from the pool.

"Angels!" cried Maude. "You're dripping water all over everything!"

"Burger you, Maude!" said the short one in a saucy way and then the Filipino bartender chased the two of them out of the room.

"Ill-bred," sighed Mrs. C. Y. Bowles.

Maude giggled and rolled his eyes. Then said to me, "Those are Rooster Van Upp's two sons. The oldest one is the smallest one and he's known as Chicken."

"Why," I asked, "were those two kids swimming this late? And why are all those people still sitting around the pool in the dark?"

"Oh, dear!" Mrs. C. Y. Bowles looked distressed. She turned to Maude. "You didn't brief him?"

"Sorry, Miranda!" Maude looked guilty and kind of worried. "You know I have no memory except for hair, where I have ninety-eight-percent perfect recollection."

Maude got up. "Come outside," said Maude to me. Gripping ahold of my arm with a hand like a hot starfish, he took me out to the pool where I could see fairly well even though the sun had gone down. *Except that the sun hadn't gone down.*

"Those people are locals," said Maude, pointing to these dozen young men and women who were lying about the pool or splashing around inside its kidney-shaped form. "They are swimming and sunning themselves. Because it's only five thirty in the afternoon."

"Maude, it's later than five thirty. It's at least seven o'clock because it's dark outside—unless I am going blind like Bette Davis in *Dark Victory*." I have got to watch out for these movie references which mean that Myra is getting ready to pounce and take the controls away—and I had a dozen oysters for dinner. Must see a doctor tomorrow about hormones. Maude says vitamin E isn't invented yet.

"No, sugar, you're not going blind. It's just that we can't see the sun and they can. They are also getting nice tans. Particularly that sexy lout over there jumping up and down on the diving board. Look at those big white varicose veins, will you? They really—what's the new phrase?—turn me on!"

42

"Maude, why is it dark for us and sunny for them?"

"Because the sun has gone down for us but it's still up there in the sky for them." Then Maude pointed one of his starfish fingers at the middle of the darkness just opposite us. "What do you see, sweetie?"

"I don't see anything because it's dark, because it's night."

"*Try* to see. Maybe I should get you some carrot juice."

I squinted and stared until, finally, I made out a huge round shape, darker than the rest of the sky and hanging up there in space like some kind of a dead planet. "I see this big round thing," I said, "and I see, well, I don't know what I see. There are these strange sorts of spirals and things in the sky."

"That's it, sweetie. Only it's not the sky you're looking at. *It's the back of the inside of the television set.*"

I guess I must've looked pretty dumb even in the dark because Maude proceeded to spell it all out for me and I thought my mind would just break open like a watch does when you drop it hard.

"The local people see the sky and the sun on this side of the Strip because they're home where they belong in 1948. But we can't see the sky and the sun because though we're here, too, we're also inside the set. Oh, really! Don't look so gloomy. Cheer up. It's fun! It's montage-time in Dixie, sweetie!"

Maude left me standing there in the darkness with the sunbathers in front of me and back of them the enormous workings of the television set that filled half the sky.

As my eyes grew accustomed to the gloom, I saw to the left of the sky what looked like this huge letter "W."

For one crazy desperate minute I thought that there was a message for me up there.

So, squinting and staring hard as I could, I was able to make out next to the "W" the letter "E."

Well, I got the message loud and clear all right. "Westinghouse."

8

Myron is asleep. Poor Myron. Nothing can save you. Not even the dozen oysters you just ate and which I have just sent on their merry way down the john after a tickle or two of the old gullet.

So we are inside the television set. Well, why not? Unfortunately, I only heard part of Maude's explanation. But then, it is with the greatest effort that I am able to look out through Myron's eyes, to tune in on what he hears. It is a bit like being at the bottom of a well when Myron is at the controls, and it takes the most intense concentration on my part to supplant him. Yet each time I return I find the trip easier; his resistance to me less. Soon he will be permanently at the bottom of the well, tastefully attired in a cement overcoat!

From the moment of my arrival I knew instinctively that Maude would be an ally. So while Myron slept or thought he was sleeping, I took control, vaulted into the saddle like Ella Raines (*Tall in the Saddle,* 1944, with John Wayne) and stole out of our room.

It was about midnight. Want to know what I did, Myron? Then try to crack *this* code, you dumb blackmun!

I am now using the same code that the Japanese used in World War II, a code which was finally broken by American intelligence, making it possible for our Navy to shoot down Admiral Yamamoto. Nevertheless that special Kamikaze Kode still remains the best of all possible codes, as I discovered while writing what many people thought was the masterpiece of the *first* Myron Breckinridge: "The Banality of Anality or *Thirty Seconds Over Tokyo*: The Gunner's View."

This startling essay did *not* appear in *Cahiers du Cinéma*, thus establishing for an entire generation the uniqueness of the original Myron's genius. Let me note in passing that I still have a sneaking fondness for the first of my metamorphoses as he slithered from art house to art house, from one 42nd Street triple-all-night feature to another. After all, out of those fructifying years came the amusing monograph "Penny Singleton and Sally Eilers: The Orality of Florality" which not even *View* would publish: proof once again that Myron's seminal— in every sense—work *had hit,* slightly to derange a metaphor, *the nail on the head.* The first Myron was also a connoisseur of the subway tearooms, and between films he could usually be found in one or another of the IRT rooms (he had a passion for the IRT), pouring.

Trial and error brought me to Maude's room on the floor above mine.

I rapped on the door.

"Come in, Harold," said Maude.

I went in, and there was Maude in a fascinating Chinese dragon gown, surrounded by a hundred wigs on plaster heads. The walls of the room are covered with photographs of celebrated women's heads with the hair highlighted.

"Who the burger is Harold?" I asked gently, all woman despite my appearance.

Maude gave me a sneaky look and giggled, "Ask me no questions . . ." Although I still don't know who Maude's swain is, we did let our hair down and had an old-fashioned hen-fest.

As I suspected, Maude is a sexual degenerate. But I make no moral judgment. Besides, fags have their uses. Were it not for the fags, man would never have flown.

The fag Leonardo da Vinci created the idea of flight, while two fag siblings (Orville and Wilbur Wright) got the human race off the ground at Kitty Hawk (a name known to every dyke). So to the fruits belong the sky! Of course, they are second-class citizens. But in my universe it is better to be second-class than to be barbarian—to be beyond the pale like those sinister heterosexuals who *breed*. Happily, by the time I am finished with them, incontinent breeding will be a thing of the past (as of 1973). After all, that is why I have returned.

For the moment I shall not divulge my master plan even in Japanese code. (I have reason to believe that the Filipino bartender is not a Filipino bartender but a Nisei spy.) I merely note in passing that I have not returned to 1948 simply to save Hollywood and the United States, amusing (and easy) as those tasks are. No, I am here to save the human race through change. For I am, let us face it once and for all, the Embodiment of Necessary Mutancy on the verge of creating a superrace, in my image.

"But first I need a wardrobe, Maude. Wigs. Eyelashes. Fingernails. Foundation garments. Adrian dresses."

Maude hooted in a most disagreeable way and it was all I could do not to smack his fat, slightly rouged cheeks. "Myron, I never knew! You're so square, yet you're—you're a drag queen!"

"Maude." I was stern as my fingers casually wrapped themselves loosely about Maude's plump toadlike neck. I saw terror in his eyes. Most suitable. *"Never* use that word to me, because I am *all woman*. Or was."

Maude gulped. "Sorry, sweetie. Do let go of my neck, Myron . . ."

"Call me Myra." I let go of his neck.

"Myra? Well, I must say this *is* a surprise . . . Myra, sweetie."

"We're going to be great friends." I was Kay Francis in *Four Jills in a Jeep*, warm, gracious; I even lisped slightly in a throaty voice as I graciously jilled.

"Natch," said Maude. "And I'll try to rustle up some duds for you. What size?"

Maude noted down my measurements.

"Now then, Maude, for the time being this is our little secret."

Maude looked puzzled. "But how can it be a secret when you're going to *wear* these clothes? Or are you just going to put them on in the closet and stay there?"

"No, keating-heel," I jeeped at him severely. "I will appear on the Strip exquisitely groomed from time to time *but* in total disguise."

"Word will get around, sweetie."

"I know. And I must take that chance. Meanwhile, there are those who must *never* know." This was awkward in the extreme. How to tell Maude that Myron must never know without telling Maude too much? Thinking hard, I tried on one of Maude's wigs in front of his special makeup mirror surrounded by electric light bulbs—perfect middle-period 20th Century Fox. I felt like June Haver but I looked, I fear, like late-period ZaSu Pitts. Hormones! Hormones!

"Maude, I am, at times, not myself."

"Then who are you?" Maude was teasing one of the wigs nervously, copying a photograph of a society queen circa Camelot.

"I have these—dizzy spells. I was having one when we met. I go on and on about how I am *Myron* Breckinridge who lives in the Valley . . ."

"Yes, sweetie, you do go on and on."

"Well, when I am in one of those 'fits,' I don't want you to mention a word to him—that is, to me—about Myra or about my wardrobe, which I am going to keep in here for the time being, if you don't mind being such an angel!" I jilled gloriously. Maude is now my slave.

We agreed to meet day after tomorrow before dinner in his room where he will have my new wardrobe assembled. I insisted on giving him Myron's gold signet ring as payment. "But you don't have to," said Maude, pocketing the ring. "We get a nice allowance once a week from Mr. Williams."

"Pawn it. I want the best, Maude. Good night, angel." I started to the door.

"Are you going to wear that wig to bed?"

"Silly me!" I jilled. I had forgotten that I was still wearing the fright wig. "By the way, who *is* Mr. Williams?"

"Such a nice man!" Yet the way Maude said that phrase I felt something was being held back. "He has a suite upstairs on the top floor."

"I shall see him tomorrow."

"Oh, I wouldn't count on that. Well, see *you* tomorrow." Maude was eager to meet his beau Harold and so I came back to this room, tripping on air. I have begun.

9

Myra has a new code, well, I will crack this one in time, too, except there will be no need as I expect to be out of here by the weekend.

So far I've got to admit this place has me stumped. For instance, this morning after breakfast I took a stroll along the highway as far as the Texaco filling station.

I said "Howdy" to the attendant and his son, who are large pink-faced men with big bellies and laugh a whole lot but you can see that they are suspicious of all of us "out-of-towners," as if everybody in California wasn't an out-of-towner including these two porkers from Ponca City, Oklahoma.

"Howdy, pardner," said the son to me as he introduced a hose full of Texaco into the rear end of what proved to be a Hudson of the kind that the Smithsonian would give a fortune for. I have, incidentally, seen *two* Kaiser-Frazer four-door sedans in apple-pie condition.

"Hi," I said and just sort of stood idly by while the porkers serviced the Hudson, all the while eyeing me as if I was about to gun them down for the contents of their dusty old-fashioned cash register.

The driver of the Hudson was a businessman-type

with a flowery tie and trousers wide enough to hide the shape of your average elephant's legs.

We fell into conversation of the usual California kind, though I made a mistake by asking about the smog-rate on the freeway that morning and of course he didn't know what I was talking about as the air back here in 1948 is just about crystal-clear and every day you can see Catalina Island if you want to look that way.

The upshot of our conversation was his agreeing to drive me into the center of Culver City where his realtor office was. I was pretty thrilled.

The Ponca City, Okla., porkers looked kind of sly when I got into the front seat beside the realtor, who revved up his Hudson which is a fine car I have always been told by those who really know. I would've given quite a few bucks to look under the hood for a while.

"The Commies," said the realtor, "are not going to stop unless we drop the big one on 'em and I say let's drop it before *they* drop it on us."

I am familiar with this conversation from having lived five years in the Valley and though I think we ought to sooner or later drop the big one on them, it is hard to do this when for all we know our President or our Vice-President or any one of a number of other good Americans might happen to be visiting in Peking or in Moscow at the time the big one went off. Of course, this is hard to explain to a realtor in Culver City back in '48. As it is, it's not easy to explain to the Young Republican League of Orange County, California, now in '73.

I agreed with the driver wholeheartedly and as we passed the two bungalows and the billboard with Gene Kelly and the three other musketeers on it, I said, "Of course, co-existence is just a dream indulged in by Com-symps . . ."

I never finished the sentence because before I knew what was happening, there was the Hudson up ahead of me, driving off into the distance, and there was I, sitting in the middle of the highway. A pickup truck which had been following us swerved to one side and the driver yelled at me to get my blackmun out of the road, which I did.

What had happened? Well, speaking technically, at the moment the Hudson crossed the barrier from where we are inside the TV to where the rest of the world is outside the TV and *Siren of Babylon,* he kept on going and I stayed where I was. That is what happened.

I brushed off my clothes and then walked as far as I could along the road toward downtown Culver City, which was not very far. First there was this glassy mirage-like effect which I have mentioned before where you can't really see anything but a sort of shining lake in the road. Then you stop. There isn't any wall or plate glass in your way. There just isn't *anything* ahead of you and you can't move an inch forward even though the locals whiz back and forth in and out of the mirage and for them there is obviously no barrier of any kind.

I was pretty depressed by all this even though it was a nice morning and the air is fresh back here and the dark clouds that are really the back of the inside of the TV set are hardly noticeable until a bit past noon when the sun drops behind the back of the TV and half the sky starts to look gloomy and shadowy and creepy—for us, that is. The locals don't notice it. I am getting to hate them.

The porker at the filling station gave me a wise look. "Decided to come on back, did you now?" The son winked at the father.

I pretended not to hear them. But I am suspicious of them and of everybody else around here. I mean, how much do they really know? Everything *looks* so normal, like the people and the cars even though they are old. Even the back lot of Metro looks perfectly O.K. with people coming and going who at a distance you can't tell if they are local or out-of-towners except sometimes the clothes will give them away.

"Hi!" On the porch of one of the bungalows was a nice-looking girl with long hair like Ann Sheridan, the Oomph Girl in *Nora Prentiss*. I've got to stop this thinking about and remembering old movies like Myra. Must also try to remember my International Code Book to see what she is up to in this phase of time.

"Hi," I said.

"You're from out-of-town, aren't you?"

"No." I was getting tired of being taken for granted by the locals. I'm from the Valley. Near Van Nuys."

"Funny. You look like one of the people who're staying at Rooster's hotel."

I knew it was my narrow trousers and not the identification disk that I wore on the chain inside my jacket, and out of view. "Yes, I'm staying at the hotel."

"Come on in. We take boarders, you know. I'm Suzy."

So I went up the step to the morning-glory-trellised porch where I found a fellow out-of-towner seated in a rocker, drinking beer. "This is Mr. Telemachus," said Suzy.

I introduced myself. Mr. Telemachus is a Greek and about thirty years old, with a deep voice and a long dead-looking face like John Carradine's: "April 1, 1968, and no jokes about April Fools' Day."

I gave my date and Suzy was delighted. "I knew you were an out-of-towner, even if you are from the Valley."

"I guess you're the latest arrival," said Mr. Telemachus. "Look forward to hearing from you tonight. There's a general meeting called. So it must be for you."

Before I could make sense of this, Suzy asked, "Would you like a beer?" She is very gracious, I'll say that. I soon learned that she hopes to get a job in wardrobe at Metro where her mother used to work as an assistant to Edith Head before her gall bladder was removed. Suzy's mother's gall bladder, that is, not Miss Head's. If the studio hadn't lost so much money last year Suzy would've been hired "but luckily this year everything looks wonderful for the studio because Mr. Mayer has hired Dore Schary who is the best there is to take over production and he's really doing a job. I know." Suzy looked proud and kind of cute in a Jean Arthur way. "I had an under-five-line part in a picture he's shooting now which is going to be a blockbuster."

"It's called *Intruder in the Dust*." Mr. Telemachus chuckled in a disagreeable way.

"Oh, Mr. Telemachus, really! How can you judge a picture before it's finished?"

"Oh, it's *finished,* Suzy."

"Now don't start talking that funny double-talk with me. *I* read the script, the whole thing, and it's about intolerance, which is a powerful subject and sure-fire box office like *Gentleman's Agreement* last year."

Suzy went for my beer. Mr. Telemachus laughed. "I know the grosses of every picture they've currently lensing at Metro. And are they in trouble!"

"You're in the Industry, aren't you?"

Mr. Telemachus nodded. "I was with daily *Variety* for six years. Then I was an executive at Four Star until I came here, with a copy of world grosses for all pix between 1930 and 1968 in my back pocket." He showed me this worn-looking book which he carries in his pocket at all times. "A tome worth its weight in gold to the locals, since it tells just what is going to happen box-office-wise to the product now lensing or prepping."

"So why don't you show it to them and get the gold?"

Mr. Telemachus' laugh was real hollow like someone

pounding a drum. "When I first got here I showed it to Suzy. I was green. She couldn't read a word. Part of the rules around here. We're not allowed to interfere. That's rule one."

At this interesting point we were interrupted by Suzy and my beer and then before we could really settle down for a visit we were interrupted again by Mrs. Connally Yarborough Bowles, who was chasing Whittaker Kaiser with a swagger stick in her hand. "Rapist!" she roared. "Foul rapist!"

For a fat man Whittaker moves very clumsily and for a frail-looking woman Mrs. Bowles is amazingly strong, but then, she is a karate brown belt as well as an expert with the swagger stick which she proceeded to us on Whittaker's fat head. He was roaring like a heifer at slaughtering time and I am sorry to say that it did us all a lot of good to see her beat the keating out of him for having taken a liberty, as she put it, with one of the maids in the hotel who had run weeping from Whittaker's room shortly after he had tried to commit an act against nature on her Mexican person early this A.M.

I didn't learn much of anything from Suzy and Mr. Telemachus except that when Mr. Williams first came here he made a lot of money on the stock market out of which our allowances are paid each Saturday. Mr. Telemachus says that though he's talked to Mr. Williams on the phone he's never met him and only Rooster Van Upp is on a first-name basis with him. Suzy remembers seeing him once when she was a little girl and she remembers him as being bald and wearing a white suit and a panama hat on the order, I suppose, of Sydney Greenstreet. Stop it, Myra!

That was a close call. She almost took charge. I was dizzy for a moment but then came to.

It's about five o'clock and I am in this awful room with the lights on though it is as dark outside for me as it is broad daylight for the Van Upp boys who are yelling and splashing in the pool below my window.

The telephone just rang and it was Mr. Williams and the conversation went about as follows.

"I trust I do not disturb you." He was very ceremonious and so was I as I told him that his trust was not in vain as I was doing nothing but staring at the wall and going crazy trying to figure out how to get the hell back home.

After some more "daresays" and "I trusts," he said, "I hope in the future you will not attempt to leave our little world by motorcar. It is not possible."

"So I found out."

"And it is demoralizing for the locals who suddenly find themselves alone in their vehicles once the barrier is passed."

"I wonder if you could have a talk with me about where we are, Mr. Williams, you and I man to man?"

"But *you* are the one who must talk to us, dear Mr. Breckinridge." Oh, he's a smooth one. "Tonight, in fact, you will address our full group in the rumpus room. That's in the basement of the hotel. Mrs. Connally Yarborough Bowles will chair the meeting and I will of course be listening in on the intercom."

"But talk about what?"

"You are the latest arrival. It is customary for the 'new boy,' as it were, to report on what has been happening since the last arrival, who, I fear, was Mr. Whittaker Kaiser. *His* report to our group was disappointing. I am sure that yours will more than compensate."

"Report on what?"

"You arrived April 17, 1973. Mr. Kaiser arrived February 9, 1973. Specifically, we would like you to tell us all that you can remember that happened in the 'other' world between February and April. You will find much interest in the sordid affair at the Watergate and a certain skepticism about Mr. Nixon's protestation of peace with honor in Vietnam."

"I happen to believe that Mr. Nixon is probably the greatest American President . . ."

"Dear Mr. Breckinridge, please! We are non-partisan. Non-sectarian. Do tell it—what is the new phrase?—*like it is*. As *you* see it. Also add any details about the arts, high fashion, cuisine. Anything, in short, that you think would amuse our group."

"How many are there?"

There was this slight, this very slight, pause on the line. "Actually we are not certain. I have kept as careful count as possible, since I am, after all, the first arrival. But a number of out-of-towners prefer making do for themselves on the back lot or in the film itself, going on and on from reel to reel. We seldom see these people. But those who do live on what we call, colloquially, the Strip, some eighty ladies and gentlemen, will be in the rumpus room at nine sharp to hear your report."

"Mr. Williams, when do we get out of here?"

"Mr. Breckinridge, what is *when?*"

"Now look here, Mr. Williams . . ."

"And where, Mr. Breckinridge, is *here? Au revoir.*"

Well, at nine o'clock the rumpus room began to fill up. Rooster Van Upp and his two sons, the tall one is fourteen and the short one is sixteen and very well-hung . . . No, Myra. You're not coming back because I had *two* dozen oysters during the day and kept them all down though I have a feeling you did get back for a few minutes during dinner when I had this funny blackout with Maude and Mrs. Connally Yarborough Bowles in the hotel dining room.

Between the oyster cocktail and the fruit-cup dessert I have no memory of what we ate or what I said except that when coffee arrived Mrs. C. Y. Bowles was staring at me with a funny expression and Maude said, "Sweetie, you are really wound up, for a Chinese caterer in the Valley." What did I say? Do? I shudder to think. But at least *she* was back no more than twenty, thirty minutes.

My eighty or so fellow prisoners of *Siren of Babylon* were all sitting on folding chairs when I went down to the rumpus room, which has no windows as it is in the basement and has overhead fluorescent lights of the same blue-gray as the television screen. By the way, the one thing we all have in common around here is missing television. Rooster keeps saying he will buy a set from Dumont, but of course even if he does there isn't anything worth watching on it and won't be for a couple of years. Meanwhile there is radio, which most of us put up with as second-best.

Otherwise there is nothing that our group has in common with each other other than our all being in this same boat together inside the TV. They are all ages, from this seventeen-year-old girl with braces on her teeth to this old man from St. Augustine, Florida, who claims to be a hundred but is probably older.

Mrs. C. Y. Bowles called the meeting to order. She then read the minutes of the last meeting which was obviously a disaster, as Whittaker Kaiser had said and perhaps done a number of violent and probably obscene things.

Mrs. C. Y. Bowles looked very grim as she reported on the meeting and everybody clucked and shook their heads and read between the lines. Whittaker looked angry but cowed—probably because Rooster Van Upp and his two boys were standing behind his chair as though ready with a series of rabbit punches to keep him in line.

Then I was introduced.

Well, I did my best to try to recall what Walter Cronkite has been telling us the last few weeks and I was surprised at how much I was able to remember. A lot of people asked questions about the Watergate and I defended our President from a number of allegations of the sort that I can't imagine any American who loves his country would allege or countenance.

It is as plain as the nose on his face that he knew nothing about those people who broke into the Democratic headquarters nor did Mr. or Mrs. Mitchell or any of his close advisers know or condone what happened. I am convinced of this.

Unfortunately, there is a small but vociferous group of radicals in our group and for a while I thought they would get out of hand but Mrs. C. Y. Bowles kept a firm leash on their emotions, and Maude's questions about hair soon relieved the tension as I did my best to recall the latest styles for fashionable women in Brentwood as glimpsed by me in the supermarket there where Mary-Ann and I sometimes shop for special things.

I also reported on the work those of us in Planned Parenthood are doing and how the young son of our neighbor in the Valley Sam Westcott Junior has just won the Nobel Prize for inventing this easy-to-take-no side-effect-permanent-style contraceptive. Sam Junior is the savior, they say, of the Third World.

Well, after these comments the meeting was warming up very nicely and Whittaker Kaiser was under control, muttering to himself but no bother to anyone, when I guess I made the gaffe of the century or of the movie anyway by saying, "Naturally I will pledge myself to help this group not only make a better America where the American dream is realized for everyone regardless of color or creed but to help each and every one of us find a way out of this movie and back home to our loved ones."

I thought this pretty rousing. Certainly I spoke from the heart with the image of Mary-Ann and the silky terriers in front of me like a vision.

Well, there was dead silence in that room. One of Maude's hairpins, if it had dropped, would have sounded like a tray of dishes.

I noticed Rooster Van Upp exchange a quick glance with his oldest and smallest son, Chicken. Whittaker Kaiser nodded drunkenly. The rest just stared at me and said nothing, nothing at all, like they hadn't heard me.

"Thank you, Mr. Breckinridge, for an excellent presentation covering those crucial weeks immediately prior to April 17, 1973, which is of course a happy date for us because *you* arrived!" There was a round of applause at the end of this very kind little speech on the part of Mrs. C. Y. Bowles and the formal part of the meeting broke up.

Rooster and sons passed around cola drinks and cookies and all sorts of people came up to me in a very friendly way to say hello and how glad they were to have me aboard and anything they could do for me they'd do and if I wanted to play bridge or poker or join the Film Discussion Society or the *Siren of Babylon* Club or whatever I was welcome to join this group or that. I must say they were very friendly except for Whittaker, who said, "You're as dumb as they are, keating-heel."

I don't know how dumb I am but I do know that I was pretty mystified by the attitude of everybody. When I asked Mrs. C. Y. Bowles if I had said something wrong, she was vague. "No, no. Certainly not. A beautiful presentation. Of course you are not yet acclimatized. That takes time. You perhaps miss—how shall I put it?—the nuances. But they will come. In good time. After all. As we say. Here. Babylon was not built. In a day." This was not much use.

Mr. Telemachus just chuckled in his bass voice. "You should do field work. Get into the movie more often. Ride the *DISSOLVES,* the *FADES,* the *CUTS.* Learn the dialogue. The secret's there, if there is one."

I mingled for a while and got to know some pleasant people of the sort that Mary-Ann and I know in the Valley and I suppose, all in all, I could hack it like the President says pretty well here for a while but only for a while.

Yet I can't help but feel that there is also something pretty strange going on. I mean even stranger than being inside *Siren of Babylon*. There is something nobody's willing to tell me.

At midnight Iris came to my room and I told her that I lost my powells in the Marine Corps at Iwo Jima. After all, I did see *Sands of Iwo Jima* a half dozen times when I was eleven, and know all the ropes.

"I don't care," she said. "Whatever's left I want."

So I gave her what was left and she went right out of her mind. Dr. Mengers has certainly done well by me. "You make Rooster look like a chipmunk!"

"That was not my intention," I said, not wanting any trouble through arousing envy of the sort that Myra's beautiful father hills used to do. But I'm afraid the word will now spread pretty fast about Dr. Mengers' handiwork and I expect I will have quite a following among the fair sex if I am so minded, which I am not, as I wish to be, as much as possible, true to Mary-Ann.

By the way, girls in 1948 are—if Iris is a good example—a bit more gamy than they are in 1973 what with Mary-Ann's geranium vaginal spray. I don't think deodorants have been invented. This is a long time ago.

10

Post Coitum Myra!

Oaf that he is, Myron collapsed after his engagement with the tacky Iris, and as he lay snoring on the bed I was able to take over the controls. You might say he blew those oysters—psychically if not physically.

It is late at night and I am in a pensive mood. For half an hour I lay on the bed whose sheets still reek of Iris's tidal process and, eyes shut, I concentrated furiously, opening one by one the attic cupboards where *my* memories are stored like so many spools of celluloid.

I played a scene here—a scene there. But soon stopped. The process was exhausting, for mine has been—I suddenly realize—a tragic life.

I realized that somber fact as I lay on the bed, fingering my flat hairy chest, trying not to look at that grotesque rehnquist which has been so ineptly sewed to what was once, literally, the symbolic center of the universe.

I confess (but only to this page) a moment's weakness. Yes, I confess to tears for all that was lost. Only by an effort of will—and will power does remain to me in vast and comforting quantities—did I throw off melancholy by forcing myself as therapy to recall the plot of Henry Hathaway's *Call Northside* 777. Then a review of

Hathaway's credits swiftly brought the roses to my electrolycised cheeks.

Thank God, no hair grows on my perfect face, while unwanted body hair will presently be banished either through hormones or—but sudden uneasy thought: do they have electrolysis back here in 1948? I seem to recall that my mother Gertrude the practical nurse removed her unwanted facial hairs with *wax*! Well, if I must endure pain in order to be beautiful, then I shall willingly dance the tarantella in my iron Maidenform bra! Perfection is all. I have never settled for less. And so to bed.

Like the phoenix, I rose from Myron's bed. I am still me. I peeked in the mirror and noted with delight that despite the inadequate frame of hair, my face is as minx-like and saucy as Kathryn Grayson's before she is contractually obliged to open her yap and give with those ear-rending high notes.

Humming to myself, I put on Myron's clothes—steeled myself to looking like a caterer by imagining that I was really Dietrich or Garbo in a butch mood circa 1933. Then I took to the Strip.

No words can describe what it is like to be back in 1948!—except my words, and I see no reason to deploy them on this page, for I have other work to do. Method is the key to all creation.

In the hotel lobby I asked Rooster Van Upp where Maude might be found and he gave me a hard look and said, "Mr. Nemo Trojan is out by the pool."

"And burger you, too!" I jilled and saw in his eyes fear as he realized that Myron the schmuck had been replaced by a force of nature capable of devastating Culver City with a single epithet.

Sitting beside the pool, guzzling daiquiris, Maude was regaling several ladies with scurrilous tales of the famous people he says that he has known. I fear Maude is something of a mythomaniac—which explains his popularity on the Strip. Lie and the world lays you!

Beside the pool lounged several youths, ranging from

well- to ill-hung. I shall get to them presently, one by one—
if not, two by two.

I was brisk. "Maude, I want to talk to you privately."

"Sweetie, I was just telling the girls what Jackie said to
me when she asked me to come stay two weeks at the
White House and de-kink her hair after what Mr. Kenneth
did to her."

"Do they know *who* you're talking about?"

"We're all post-1960," said one of the ladies. "Fact,
we have a Post-Sixty Club and if you'd like . . ."

A phrase or two—nothing worth recording—and the
girls fled, leaving Maude with that look on his face I have
come to know so well. It is like that of Miriam Hopkins
when she first gets a gander of Frederic March as he
turns into quaint, crusty Mr. Hyde.

"So it's you, Myra," said Maude. "Well, I got most of
your wardrobe."

"You angel!"

"I must say it's very funny, the way you're two people."

"One and a half, Maude. And Myron is the half that is
about to go."

Clothes-wise Maude came through splendidly.

"The quality is not the best," I said, arranging the
snood to cover my auburn wig, which consists of a high
pompadour in the front with a long Ann Sheridan fall in
the back. "But the overall effect is"—I rolled my eyes like
Ann Dvorak—"devastating!"

"Sweetie, you have to be seen to be believed!" Maude
was even more thrilled than I at the transformation in
front of his middle-period 20th Century-Fox mirror.

"Now all that we need do is rebuild my father hills and
cut off this hideous rehnquist."

"Oh, Myra, not that!" Maude's greedy—and highly
unbecoming—interest in Dr. Mengers' Frankenstein
monster forced me to be sharp. "Look but don't touch," I
said sternly. Then when I saw Maude's face crinkle with
disappointment, I relented. "If you like, I'll give it to you
when it's been removed!"

Maude shuddered. "Myra, you couldn't? You wouldn't! You *mustn't*!"

But I was already looking up plastic surgeons in the Culver City yellow pages. Apparently there are only two. One did not answer. The other was on vacation at Lake Arrowhead but will be back in a few days. "Next June 1— in three weeks—when the picture starts shooting again, I shall have the operation performed right here in the hotel."

"Sugar, no surgeon worth his salt is going to make a house call."

But I know all the difficulties and will, as always, surmount them. I have a hunch that silicone has not yet been invented, but fortunately, *I remember the formula.* Incidentally, there is no reason why I cannot make a fortune back here where there must be thousands of transsexualists longing to be properly father-hilled. By cornering the market in silicone . . . No! I have more important work.

Maude suggested that we have a drink at the Mannix Motel bar. "A sort of trial run, sugar. To see if you're recognized. Also, there are usually some really super studs at the Mannix."

"Maude, you are an insatiable pervert!" I jilled, amused at Maude's passion for males of the lower order.

The Mannix bar was—how shall I describe it? Funky. Smelling of beer and pre-filter cigarette smoke and that funny odor that is 1948 and perfectly indescribable in the vocabulary of 1973. The inevitable jukebox played "Sentimental Journey." The locals can never get enough of that oldie.

We sat at the booth farthest from the jukebox and ordered one of Eddie Mannix's special Sazerac cocktails (this Eddie Mannix is no relation to Eddie Mannix the top-flight Metro executive). As I suspected, there were no super studs or even studs in the bar; a lackluster group of locals with a sprinkling of out-of-towners. No one recognized me. Not even Whittaker Kaiser, who actually gave me the eye—if that tiny red oyster so like to an infected buttonhole could be said to have any *interpretable* expression. He shall be dealt with in good time.

"Maude, I've got to get onto the Metro lot."

"Sweetie, just fly across the Strip and there you are!"

"No. I want to go to the front office. I want to meet Louis B. Mayer and Dore Schary." I did not tell Maude that I have decided to become, briefly, for the experience only, a movie star, on my own terms of course. A half mill up front. A percentage of the gross. Terms that are unknown back here but I am by definition *avant-garde*, particularly in the past.

"You have got to be kidding, sugar. Even if they were to put you under contract, there's no way of your getting from here to there."

"Then we must work out a compromise." I was all sweet reason and lovely logic in perfect Virginia Bruce balance. Virginia must now, even as I write, be filming *Night Has a Thousand Eyes*. Did she find happiness with that Turk she married? And why, if she was mad for Turks, didn't she marry adorable Turhan Bey, now a photographer in Vienna? Questions, questions!

"The studio chiefs can always come *here* for conferences. Have you met any of them, by the way?"

"Met them? Sweetie, I've done Mrs. Dore Schary's hair a dozen times. She rings me from their palatial Bel Air mansion and says, 'Maude, my hair needs bending,' and I say, 'Come right over, Miriam,' and as I tend to her in my room we discuss her paintings—she's *talented*! And of course we talk about all the problems between Dore and L. B. which are, let me tell you, coming to a head . . ."

I was suddenly aware in the midst of Maude's deliciously spontaneous lie (he no more knows Miriam Schary than I do) that a young man of extraordinary allure had come into the bar. "Gimme a brew!" he commanded.

Beneath my half-lowered beaded lashes, I took inventory: old checked shirt, Levis faded to no color, a silver Indian belt, worn moccasins, dingy white socks of the sort affected by working-class youths in every generation.

Gray eyes, black hair, bronzed skin, whilst at the denim crotch a hornet's nest of sheerest menace to the future. He turned his back to me. Oh, those globes. No! Those gorgeous hemispheres, crying out to be wrenched apart in order that one might create the opposite to Plato's beast by substituting that dumb Greek's trendy ideal of the un-natural whole to my truer vision of forcibly divided and forever separated parts. No monist Myra!

"Hey," said the youth to Maude. Apparently he is half Cherokee Indian (the upper half, Maude swore to me, since the lower half of your average brave need not cause mother to sprint to the letter box for news of what is sel-dom more than a darkling shrimp despite that race's hero-ism at Wounded Knee best represented by the superb mimesis of Jeff Chandler as Cochise in *Broken Arrow*).

Half-Cherokee is a lineman with the telephone company and according to Maude strictly "jam," a word new to me but much in use back here to describe those males so addicted to heterosexuality that they will not drop their drawers for another male no matter how high the price—under twenty dollars, that is. During my formative pre-Myra years, as Myron the First, I came to the cynical conclusion that every working-class youth has his price, which varies from practically nothing to all for the re-leased of seminal fluids in a friendly moist orifice to a fair chunk of cash if the fudge to be stirred is his.

Half-Cherokee plainly dislikes Maude and fags in gen-eral, but as for me . . .

"I gotta tell you, Myra, I never seen a woman like you before." His sinewy thigh was jammed against mine un-der the table, his moccasined foot was delicately tickling my ankle straps; he was so close that I could smell his rich, slightly musky odor, like Romanoff caviar newly spread on a Triscuit with a dash of lemon juice, a soup-çon of onion.

Maude was delighted and, perhaps, just the tiniest bit jealous of my success with Half-Cherokee. "He's never been with a fag, have you, Butch?"

Half-Cherokee finished his beer with a provocative long

suck. "No, sir, and I ain't startin' now. Hell, in the Marines at Pendleton, they was selling their blackmuns for ten bucks a throw—but not yours truly! I was always saving up for a good broad. Like you, Myra."

"I hope there's plenty in the bank now!" I fear that I allowed my voice to take on the tonality of the sinister Mae West.

"I reckon I could drown you," he said quietly, again pushing his thigh against mine, to which I responded by reaching under the table and taking into my hand his entire posterity (the meat was mashed in with the potatoes). He looked shocked. Before he could wriggle away, I gave a powerful squeeze. He choked, as though the wind had just been knocked out of him, which, symbolically at least, it had.

"Jesus!" He gaped at me.

"What's the matter?" Maude had seen nothing.

"I'm just teasing Half-Cherokee." I was Joan Leslie winsome.

Poor stud, he did not know what to make of my sudden assault. Yet still he wants me even though pain is obviously not his bag; nor is it mine for that matter, except as catharsis, as a means of revelation. It was then that I had *my* revelation.

As I sit in this depressing hotel room (a cabin at the Mannix is plainly in the cards) I realize that once again fate has been my patsy. Half-Cherokee will be my first creation!

When I was Myra Breckinridge, the goddess of the late sixties and symbol of all that was best in Hollywood, I began, blindly, I confess, my restructuring of the sexes. Through the anal penetration of what that son of a bitch my uncle Buck Loner used to call your average hundred-percent all-American stud, I shifted the self-image of one Rusty Godowsky (boyfriend to the dread Mary-Ann) from bull to heifer. With a single gesture I was able, once and for all, to shatter the false machismo of the American male. As the world now knows, my total victory over Rusty, et al., put an end not only to the American conquest of Asia but to the previously undisputed primacy of the combustion engine.

Unhappily, my creation of Unisex proved to be no more than a stopgap. I did not go far enough (except with myself and, *mea culpa,* I humbly confess that when I made myself Myra Breckinridge, I did so simply in order to be unique). I realize now that in my petty selfishness I was deliberately denying others what I was so quick to claim as my own *rebirth-rite.* Worse, it is now evident that I have doomed the entire human race to death from famine and pestilence as the result of over-population because, thanks to my efforts, the American male now lacks the arrogant sexual thrust to conduct those wars that in the past were so necessary to population control through the playful use of anti-personnel weaponry. Yet the American male—like all males—still continues mindlessly to reproduce. I made him spiritual heifer but not *total* heifer. In a nutshell, I *un*manned the American male when I should have *de*manned him.

Sitting there in the Mannix bar, my hand squeezing Half-Cherokee's powells (in which I could feel a billion Half-Cherokee spermatozoa writhing in their eagerness to make a billion Quarter-Cherokee ready to eat up the last of the world's diminishing food supply), I realized what I must do. *I must remove those powells—darkling shrimp, too.*

But obviously that is only the beginning. Something new, vital, must take the place of this sturdy lineman once he is rid of his lethal genitalia. Therefore, I shall, solemnly, share with him my glory—with the whole world, for that matter. I am in a *giving* mood! I shall pump silicone into Half-Cherokee's tiny father hills and introduce female hormones into his bloodstream. Then, after a crash course in makeup and skin care, I shall present him to a grateful world as a gorgeous, fun-loving, sterile Amazon, an Indian princess made for good times but not for breeding.

A few press conferences, perhaps a lecture tour of the major cities, a documentary film and my fun-loving sterile

Amazon will be the ideal of every red-blooded American boy. Something to emulate. Population will then decrease at such a rate that by 1973 we should see the human race in perfect harmony with the environment, while, best of all, we shall be living in a joyous world dominated by fun-loving sterile Amazons, at peace with one another and the Arab emirates.

I have just sent President Truman a telegram saying that the Korean War must be called off. It will not be necessary, as I am about to stabilize world population. Naturally, a small cadre of unrestructured men and women will be allowed to breed. The rest of the men, however, will be re-created in my image! If I may say so, selflessness on this scale is unique in human history, and smacks of the divine.

Tomorrow I shall buy the basic ingredients for silicone, as well as a book on surgery. The whole thing could not be simpler. Three quick slices, tie up the loose ends and start pumping.

But, first, physician, heal thyself!

11

I got up early this A.M. to find that my face was covered with makeup and that Myra had gone to bed wearing these god-awful false eyelashes which I have flushed down the toilet. Also, Myra has *tweezered* my eyebrows! You whizzer white, if I ever get my hands on you it will be murder, justifiable homicide as any court would agree.

Today is my day to get out of here and I think the way out is somewhere around where I came in.

At breakfast in the hotel Mr. Telemachus happened to come in and offered to show me around the back lot. "Some interesting people are living there. Might give you a few ideas."

"Morning, Mac," said Mr. Telemachus to the guard at the gate who was reading another *Hollywood Reporter*.

"Morning, Abner," said the guard and motioned us through.

"Is that your name—Abner?" I asked.

"No. But that's what he thinks it is."

"He sees us, doesn't he?"

"He sees something but maybe it's not us. Maybe it's Abner." This was all pretty obscure. Mr. Telemachus likes his little mystery, which I don't.

Beyond the gate to the lot there is a street which used to be used for the Andy Hardy movies. It is a wide curving street with real lawns in front of the false-front houses and real trees. Every day real gardeners tend the lawns and prune the trees and the bushes as though this were all part of someone's private estate.

"That's Judge Hardy's house." Mr. Telemachus showed me all the sights but I couldn't've cared less since all I really want to know is where the nearest exit is.

"How," I said, sounding as casual as I could as we wandered along the Hardy street, "do you—uh, get out of here? You know, back to where we came from?"

Mr. Telemachus acted like he hadn't heard me. "The last Hardy film," he said, "was released last year. It bombed."

"No." I surprised myself—well, not really. Myra's down there sending me all sorts of god-awful messages. I couldn't stop myself from saying, "They'll make one more in 1957."

I also couldn't stop myself from remembering the marquee blazing with *Andy Hardy Comes Home,* and me standing under it with, I'm sorry to report, this heavy eye makeup and bee-stung crimson lips and a trench coat like Marlene Dietrich. It was the start of Myra, really, that year when I was Myron first time around—a fag, I guess you'd have to say—and sent my first essay to André Bazin at *Cahiers du Cinéma* on Garbo's teeth and how dramatically they changed after *As You Desire Me.* André Bazin died before he could write back his view on this subject.

"They'll lose their shirt, too. Nobody wants that crapola any more." Mr. Telemachus gave me from memory the disastrous worldwide grosses of Metro's last Hardy movie as well as the grosses of all films the studio is currently (1948) making. "Biggest bust of all will be *Siren of Babylon.* Domestic gross one million two. Negative cost one million three."

The back lot is a pretty big place, a good many acres of woods and streams and sets—city streets, French villages, old mansions, with these tourists riding in funny sort of trolley cars, seeing the sights sort of like they do now at Universal City. Yet all the while, back of everything, there is this giant screen hanging like in a drive-in movie against the blue-gray sky with the figures of Maria Montez and Bruce Cabot slowly acting out *Siren of Babylon* backwards from where we are. We out-of-towners see it. The locals don't . . .

12

Curious that Myron cannot get the point to where we are. He even misses the point to time and its simultaneity. Well, I shall not explain it to him—even if I could, which I cannot.

The bastard flushed my eyelashes down the toilet! He will pay for this. I confess, however, if only to this Kamikaze Kode, that I am somewhat disturbed at Myron's recuperative powers. *He keeps coming back.* Although his search for hormones has been as fruitless as my own (I have a lead, however, in Brentwood), he simply will not stay put. My terror is that he will blunder onto the exit, so clearly marked. If he does, I will kill him rather than face a life in the San Fernando Valley with Mary-Ann, Watergate, recession and Peckinpah. Call it suicide, I don't care.

Meanwhile, I have been active on a number of fronts. I have bought (or acquired on the back lot) disinfectant, a scalpel, a hypodermic needle, sutures. The components for silicone are now nicely jelling in a bucket in Maude's closet.

"What on earth do you want all those *sinister* things for?"

"Ask me no questions . . ." I jilled a reprise of

74

Maude's favorite line. Actually, if Maude would tell fewer lies people would ask him fewer questions.

So far I have been able to come and go pretty much unnoticed in the hotel, though I can see that Rooster is puzzled to have observed, on at least two occasions, a strange and wondrously beautiful girl coming downstairs from the bedrooms. Luckily, each time I was in the company of Maude, who is above suspicion in that department.

Even before tonight—this marvelous evening—I had decided that the time had come to take a cabin at the Mannix Motel: a *pied-à-terre*—a home away from Myron. Also the isolation of one of the Mannix cabins will provide an ideal operating room for the Culver City surgeon —and for me!

"Hello, gorgeous!" It was Eddie Mannix himself who greeted me. Old, randy, drunk, Mannix is a true Californian from New York. I threw the full voltage of my charm at him.

"Gorgeous yourself, you hunk of man! Victor Mature has nothing on you, big boy!" I should note that a day or two ago while examining Myron's memory bank—soon to be in the hands of the receivers— I was saddened to find that Victor Mature (whose photograph taken unaware in the altogether during his heroic service in World War II helped defeat Hitler, Mussolini and Tojo) acted not long ago in an *Italian* film, directed by a one-time bad actor and neo-realismo director, with a script by a Broadway jokster. Worse, in the course of this travesty, the *image of Victor Mature was deliberately mocked*! I am certain that with some judicious tinkering back here, I shall be able to save Victor from his subsequent decline into camp even though, as I write these lines in Japanese, Victor has been taking a wrong turn in his career, collecting "kudos," as Mr. Telemachus would say, for such "serioso" products as *I Wake Up Screaming.* Admittedly, Victor is currently lensing *Samson and Delilah,* a film in which his father hills will be revealed to an astonished world as larger and more significant than those of co-star Hedy Lamarr—a cataclysmic reversal of the expected which presaged my own subsequent—and still unfinished—realignment of the sexes.

Unfortunately, in the pre-Myra world, Victor's triumph in *Samson and Delilah* proved to be a one-shot affair. Post-Myra, Victor must now play the title role in the remake of *Ben-Hur.* If he does, I guarantee that in the seventies he will be a star greater than *Last Brando in Paris,* with or without the two fingers up his blackmun (question to ask the makers of that deeply sentimental film [closer to *Snow White and the Seven Dwarfs* than to say, *The Egyptian*]: were the fingernails of the poodlesque girl *actually* trimmed? Of course, I have only Myron's recollection of the film to go on, and perhaps there are essential points he missed, as usual).

"Big boy," I addressed Eddie Mannix with moistened lips half ajar like poor Veronica Lake now working as a luncheonette hostess and barmaid, glorious platinum locks long since shorn. "I may want to move over here, to be close to *you.*"

"Any time, sweetheart." Mannix pinched my right hip and it was all I could do not to throw him through the window. In this world of her creation, it is Myra Breckinridge who pinches. But by playing it cool, I was rewarded with the key to Cabin 9—the most isolated cabin of all, he assured me with a wink. Then I went into the bar.

Half-Cherokee was sitting by the jukebox, arms back of his head, moccasined feet on a chair, eyes shut, listening to "Sentimental Journey," a beer in front of him—the picture of masculine contentment, ready to be altered entirely by the hand of the master potter.

As I joined Half-Cherokee, he gave me a long look—and I could not help but think how beautiful those gray eyes will look with false eyelashes and the thick brows that grow together in a straight line plucked.

"Have a brew, Myra."

I had a brew. I was enchanting. Seductive. Infatuating.

76

Frilly, yes, and feminine in the pre-Lib way. Everything a manly boy would want a girl—*his* girl—to be.

I encouraged him to talk about himself. "I just broke up with this girl. Pussy. Yeah, that's her name, believe it or not. She's Irish and real fair like you. But she wants to marry and settle down and me I want to like play the field. Not that I'm against getting married. I'd like that when I'm getting old like thirty. Yeah, I'd like it then. To settle down and have five or six kids."

With some effort I contained my disgust. If ever anyone was needed, I am needed at this crossroads in human history. As we sat there, I could almost hear the cries of the nearly sixty babies born every minute on this crowded globe as of 1948. Today (1973) it is closer to two hundred a minute unless I succeed in getting to the root of the matter. Whether I prevail or not—and I know that all the prayers of the human race are with me, and thank you all—I can guarantee that at least one Half-Cherokee will not add to the starving billions of the seventies.

I softened him up. Then heated him up in order to string him along—but cautiously (I thought) since I am not yet fully equipped to re-create him. Half-Cherokee's lust, however, was so great that I was tempted to play with him as matador does with bull. I fear I was naughty.

"Why don't we go up to your place, Myra?" Under the table a strong hot hand held my upper thigh.

"Oh, I couldn't. Not at the Thalberg! Think of my rep! That's all a girl has."

"You got a key to one of ole Eddie's cabins. I saw you take it."

"What sharp eyes you have!"

Half-Cherokee was now seriously aroused. I was seriously amused and thought, oh, for heaven's sake, you silly billy! What have you got to lose? If he becomes too forward, you have the means to bring him to heel.

And so I committed my near-fatal error. I left the bar. Ten minutes later he left the bar. One minute later we were together in the cabin farthest from the road, and from help.

I was not prepared for his crudeness, his violence.

No sooner had Half-Cherokee locked the door behind him than I saw an expression on his face which, I confess, I did not like. Gone was the hot pleading boy of only eleven minutes earlier. Instead there was the contorted face of a man with rape on his mind.

Roughly he grabbed me. Oh dear, I thought wearily. Has it come to this? I asked myself, echoing James Mason as he played the Emperor Franz Josef in the Terence Young remake of *Mayerling*, a film that has, I gather, delighted hundreds of long-distance jet-travelers, amongst them Myron.

"Baby, I gotta have it. And I gotta have it now!"

"Please," I whispered, gently pushing at his hard chest which was jammed against my Maidenform bra stuffed with latex. But his only response was to slam his hornet's nest (considerably enlarged) against my crotch.

I struggled. He held my arms close to my sides. He was very strong, I noted. For one weak but delicious moment as I inhaled the clean sweat of his body, I weighed the pros and cons of surrender. But when his greedy lips began to ravish my ear and I realized that my wig might fall off, I wrenched free of him.

"Come here," he commanded.

"No, no!" I fluttered away. "I'm saving myself for Mr. Right."

"Honey, *I'm* Mr. Right." He started toward me, an ominous figure.

"But I don't *know* you. I mean let's not hurry this, darling. This is only our first real date. Petting, yes, but not . . ."

He grabbed me. I leapt behind the bed.

"Keating!" He swore. "Come here, bitch!"

"Darling, no. Please. I want you to respect me." To my joy I realized that vocally I had, for the first time, achieved the dark throaty Margaret Sullavan quality.

Transfixed by the sound of my own magical voice, I fear
I let down my guard.

Half-Cherokee dove across the bed and tackled me.
Yes, tackled *Myra Breckinridge,* a goddess, true, but also
a woman, tender, frail. I was stunned by his force; hor-
rified by his brutality; saddened that he did not respect
me.

For a confused moment he held me pinioned in his
arms, my back pressed against the radiator which left me
—I just noticed—with a black and blue derrière. I looked
up; saw a satanic smile. "I'm gonna burger you, bitch."
Those carven boyish lips were like a satyr's, no, like a
carnivore's.

"Don't, please!" Without difficulty I summoned a tear
to my eye. After all, Margaret Sullavan's voice was coming from *me.*

"You white bitches are all alike, rehnquist-teasers."

I was bemused by the adjective. It was not *me* he
wanted—beautiful and vulnerable as I am. No, it was a
white woman that he wanted to humiliate. He wanted to
avenge Wounded Knee in my body. At that instant, I fear,
the lad lost my sympathy if not my interest.

As he started to rip at my dress, I gave him my special
Giant Moth karate blow to the belly. He doubled up, unable to breathe. Then a well-aimed twist and push (co-
ordinating right shoulder with left leg), dropped him to
the floor with a crash.

Before he knew what hit him, I was seated on the
small of his back with his left arm twisted behind him so
that the slightest pressure of my forefinger on his wrist
would cause the most excruciating pain.

"Christ!" he grunted. "What the burger do you think
you're doing?"

"Protecting myself from rape—darling."

"Rape, keating!" he snarled into the floor, still un-
broken. "You want it. You know you want it."

"Not—perhaps—in the way you think." Delicately I
pressed my forefinger on his wrist and was rewarded
with a yelp.

"Stop that!"

"Only if you promise to be a good boy."

"What're you? Some kinda freak? A lady wrestler or something?" He looked at me over his shoulder. For the first time I detected the beginning of fear. But I had—have —no desire to hurt him. I want only to rebuild him in my own image. I also knew that if I were to frighten him too much he would never return.

"Foolish goose!" I gave him a sweet smile. "I just learned a few little tricks to keep from being all mussed up by purse-snatchers and by rapists."

"But you want it, Myra. I know you do. Hey, come on. Let me up, and I'll show you a good time."

"That I'd like to see, darling. But I think you better cool off a bit." I made myself comfortable on his firm rubbery buttocks. He looked remarkably appealing with his head twisted around so that he could see me like the new moon over his left shoulder, the straight black hair all tousled. I noticed that in our scuffle he had lost his moccasins.

One associative thought led to another. "You called me a white bitch."

"Well, you are. I mean you're white."

Pressure no greater than a feather's fall on his wrist. "Don't!" He yelled.

"Say you're sorry for calling me a bitch, darling."

"I'm sorry."

"That's a good boy. You hate white people, don't you?"

"No. Hell, I'm half white."

"Let's see which half."

He stared at me blankly.

With my right hand I took his right ankle and bent his leg back so that the large square foot in its dingy white sock was almost level with my eyes. I peeled off the damp sock.

"What're you doing?" He tried to straighten his leg but pressure on the wrist made him change his mind. He groaned. Then shuddered as I examined the calloused olive-tinted sole of his foot.

"Looking to see what color you really are. Darkies have pink soles."

"I ain't no nigger," he muttered.

"No, but the bottom of your foot is lighter than the rest. You're definitely two-toned, darling!" This was quite true. He was not, literally, a redskin—more light brown with yellowish tints. I noticed that the hairs on his ankle were sparse, black and fine.

"Come on," he said, embarrassed as I playfully tickled his toes. "Let me up. Let's call it a day. I'm sorry what I did."

I was now tickling the other foot, and he began to shudder. "Hey, stop! I'm ticklish."

I stopped. "Let's see if you're two-toned everywhere." I reached under him and got his belt buckle in my hand. He tried to roll away from me. This time I gave him sufficient pressure to make him scream.

"Darling, there must be no secrets between us." I changed my position; sat on his shoulder blades.

"You're breaking my arm," he whined.

I was also pushing his jeans down to his knees with my foot. He wore no underwear. The smooth coppery buttocks glistened sweatily in the bright glare of the single overhead Mazda.

"Well, well," I said significantly.

"Well, well . . . what?" He squeaked, nervously clenching his buttocks tight together.

I ran my hand lightly over the silky moist surface; it was like a hard Goodyear rubber tire. "Relax, darling." My hand was at the juncture of buttocks and legs, a dark, velvety Maltese cross that marked the spot, as it were: the center of the male, the sacred blackmun.

"I *am* relaxed. Listen. I better get going."

I gave his bottom a little smack. "Open for Myra."

"For Christ's sake . . ."

Pressure on the wrist; a cry; the buttocks went slack. I pushed at them; made them jiggle. Although at present his musculature is typically masculine, I could see how, once his male organs are removed and his system fortified with female hormones, the broad pelvic region would be truly ravishing.

Absence of unsightly hairs on his back (except for a single black tuft at the beginning of the anus) is also a definite plus. Looking down at what will soon be a woman's superb thighs, I could not help but think how one day some man—no, a host of men!—will be forever in my debt when they hold in their arms the luscious woman's body of Half-Cherokee, my creation.

But I still have my work cut out for me. "Spread your legs wide, darling."

"Keating!" He moaned but obeyed. There on the floor, vulnerable yet somehow impressive, were his large black hairless powells.

"What a nice bean-bag!" I sounded like Marie Wilson in a Ken Murray sketch. I gathered the two powells in my hand, and again was appalled at nature's terrible mindless fecundity. "Just think of all the billions of little Half-Cherokees swimming around in there, waiting to get out."

"Not now they aren't." (I had broken him.) "Come on. Let me up."

"But maybe I've changed *my* mind." I teased him. "Maybe I want it now."

"I don't think I can."

"Some stud! Anyway, you need relief, darling. All rapists do."

I got off him suddenly. "Stand up, darling."

Warily he got to his feet. He looked frightened and angry, as what would-be rapist would not with his trousers about his ankles and his shirt hiked up to his armpits?

"You can relieve yourself, darling," I said, pointing to his dark long rehnquist which curved in a baroque line over the loose-hanging powells. He was not circumcised. I was also pleased to note that except for a silky black mustache at the base of the rehnquist, his front was as hairless as his back. I was particularly satisfied by the nipples: they are small, brown and for a male unusually protuberant, almost a quarter inch in length when excited. I know, for I proceeded to tickle him as he stood there dumbly, unable to believe what was happening to him.

"There's many a girl who would love to have father hills like yours."

"I ain't got father hills."

I slapped the hard flat pectoral muscle with my hand. "But, darling, you do have beautiful, exciting, excitable nipples." As I played with him I studied the veins near his armpit, trying to recall which is the one that will take the silicone. I must get the old anatomy book out and do my homework.

As a reward for Half-Cherokee's new cooperativeness, I allowed him to masturbate in front of me. At first he was shy; even hostile. But with a sharp word or two I was able to persuade him to do what I wanted him to do.

During the milking process, my thoughts were somber. Three times in forty-two minutes I forced him to shoot into the world billions of Half-Cherokees. "Jesus, I can't do it again this quick," he whimpered after the second full flooding that hurtled toward the bed where I was sitting, falling to the floor like a thick deadly white rain.

"I can't . . . any more." His breath was coming in great gasps; his face and armpits were streaked with sweat. He held tight his powells in one hand as though to protect them from me (I have already decided where the first incision will be in his groin).

As I write, I can imagine the joy I shall experience when I detach that dark lethal bag from the beautiful and *sterile* Amazon, the Indian princess who is waiting for me to bring her into the world. I shall christen her Minnehaha.

It is plain that nature and I are on a collision course. Happily, nature is at a disadvantage, for nature is mindless and I am pure mind. Wanting to preserve our species, nature idiotically made us able to breed at much too early an age and in too vast quantities. As a result of nature's mismanagement, any male in his lifetime can personally produce 43,800 children, using a different woman of course for each child. With the use of artificial insemination, a healthy male could double the world's population after a few hours of idle handwork of the sort I required Half-Cherokee to perform.

This must stop.

The balance between population and food supply is now undone. Starvation has begun in the Third World. According to FAO, if all the world's arable land were properly farmed and the food was then equally distributed, there would be sufficient calories for the three billion people now alive *but* there would be insufficient protein per capita. Result? Malnutrition for all.

I alone can save the human race. Knowing what I know, and given this miraculous opportunity to begin the reduction of population in 1948 by creating a new and exciting human image, one that every healthy boy will want to imitate, I shall be able in one generation to reduce the world's population to *minus* zero growth—and all in the name of metamorphosis and of joy!

As Half-Cherokee toweled his body and then cleaned up the mess he had made on the floor, I stared at him with half-shut eyes, saw him as a woman, saw the thick musculature of arms and thighs reduced by hormones to soft suppleness; envisaged father hills like those of one of Gauguin's native girls (the suicide of George Sanders was an act of self-definition equal to my own; and all honor to one who found it better to be dead than bored); while the dark dangling threat to the race's future would be sliced away, and buried deep (*you'll* get no child, oh, mandrake root!).

I am already planning the press conference we will hold. Half-Cherokee—beautifully groomed by Edith Head—will address the members of the fourth estate, explaining to them the whys and wherefores of the metamorphosis (with perhaps a modest phrase or two from me). Then Minnehaha will offer herself as a living solution to the problem of overpopulation (not to mention this century's restless search for sexual identity), and together we will open a clinic, no, a thousand clinics all around the world in order to create an entire race of beautiful, sterile, fun-loving Amazons.

In no time at all, Half-Cherokee had put on his clothes; had run to the door, as though fearful I might stop him. But how could I—when I was suddenly June Allyson, twinkling my eyes and husking my voice?

"I have great plans for you, darling."

"I bet." His shaky fingers fumbled with the doorknob.

I stepped toward him; he jumped backward, one hand protecting his crotch, the other his face. Poor boy! I fear he has overracted to me.

"Don't be afraid, darling." I touched his cheek to make sure that he has no beard. Except for a bit of stubble under the chin, the boy's face is as smooth as Dolores del Rio's. I fear that I am already half in love with my raw material. "Next time I'll have a wonderful present for you."

"How about that?" He was shaking in his moccasins. I patted his cheek.

"Sayonara," I husked, and let him run off into the night. Two minutes later I heard his motorcycle revving up. A blast. He was gone.

I note in the mirror that my eyes are luminous with the power that has begun to concentrate in me. Yet in my victory I am, as always, pensive, self-critical. It is not for my sake but for that of our dying race that I must now, quite simply, bring nature to her knees in order that there be sufficient food and space for those who wish to live with dignity on this turning green globe whose protectress I am.

I shall now move all my equipment into this motel cabin, where, I pray, Myron will never set foot. He will remain in his digs at the Thalberg Hotel. I at the Mannix, where, as Maude would say, "There's always room."

13

O.K., Myra, so you are taking over for a day or two at a time now but it's the war not the battle that matters and I am winning the war though I can't say I like waking up every morning with my face smeared with inches of makeup. When I find your drag, you whizzer white, I am going to tear it to pieces.

Rooster Van Upp's oldest son Chicken brought me coffee this morning after I had cleaned up my face. Chicken was wearing blue jeans and Keds and a Hawaiian shirt. He has a crewcut which looks like golden fuzz on his round thick head. As he put the tray down I could see inside his short sleeve where the armpit is, and the hairs in there are just as golden if fewer than the ones on his head and beaded with these tiny drops of sweat. "Hot day," says Chicken.

Now why did I keep on staring at Chicken like that when I am not a fag but straight as a die with the best little wife in the Valley? I know why. It is because Myra is all over the place. This is going to stop. You hear me?

Thank God, we were interrupted by Maude, who came in the room with this package and when Chicken saw Maude he skedaddled out of the room. Flaming queens like Maude often have that effect on impressionable adolescents in Southern California who even when they like getting blown by said queens are terrified of a daiquiri-tasting tongue landing in their ear or up their . . .

I am getting double vision as I write these lines. It's like being caught in one of *Siren of Babylon's* lap-dissolves. There. Now it's gone.

"Good morning, sweetie!" Maude was in a very good humor. "You don't look so good. What you need is some action. Like Chicken Van Upp maybe?" Maude leered.

"You must be crazy, Maude . . ." I began.

"Well, I got you a different wig. And more clothes." Maude undid the package and there inside was this complete forties hooker outfit, consisting of a flashy short dress with the Adrian shoulders, ankle-strap black patent leather stiletto-heeled shoes, foundation garments of the sort which make any normal man hard as a rock, and a black wig.

"What the burger," I asked, "is all this?"

"Sorry, Myra," Maude stammered, "I mean *Myron*. It's nothing at all. Forget I ever came by." Maude swept the clothes display back into this bag.

"You thought I was Myra, didn't you?" I was mean as all hell. "You're in cahoots with that bitch."

Maude sniffed. "Myra is a good friend, and I won't hear a word against her from the likes of you."

"You keep her drag for her, don't you?"

"Ask me no questions, I'll tell you no lies." And Maude was out of the room.

I got dressed and headed for the back lot. I am going, all by myself, back to the beginning. Back to where I came in. I am getting out of this movie.

14

Myron took control for half a day in which, I gather, he managed to antagonize everyone. He also went onto the back lot but, thank God, did not manage to find the exit. Sooner or later of course he will, as it is plainly marked, according to the Fire Laws. I must move fast.

I met Maude in the bar of the Mannix, where we had an apéritif as we waited for Half-Cherokee. At last I was ready for him.

I have converted my cabin into an operating room. Ready are the scalpel, the sutures, the clamps, the book of anatomy (belonging to Eddie Mannix, who is a darling but something of a hypochondriac) and of course a gallon of Lysol. The silicone has jelled nicely in its plastic bucket and I now have more than enough to father-hill Half-Cherokee to Marie Wilson proportions. I have also obtained four sets of handcuffs (lifted from the Police Station Set on the back lot), as well as a tin of ether used by the housekeeper at the Thalberg to clean rugs.

I have not yet made up my mind whether or not Half-Cherokee should be conscious or not during the operation. It would be a vivid experience for him to say *aloha* to his old sex and *ciao* to his new sex. After all, I was given nothing stronger than Demerol when I underwent transformation in Copenhagen, and not only did I feel no pain, I experienced ecstasy as I watched the longed-for removal. But I fear that Half-Cherokee is the sort of sensitive young rapist who would burst into tears at the slightest prick, so I shall probably have to put him to sleep.

"I think," giggled Maude, "that Myron is gay."

"I dislike that world, Maude." There was a threat of jeep in my voice that was plainly Carole Landis' to any aficionado.

"You may not like the word, Myra, but I saw the *way* Myron was staring at Chicken Van Upp."

"Myron is much too dull for anything so interesting. Not that the lobotomized Chicken is exactly interesting except as a morbid example of how California grows its boys like navel oranges, only instead of lacking pits they lack wits."

"I heard that, Breckinridge." It was Whittaker Kaiser, who has, somehow, learned that I am, on occasion, the monster Myron.

Whittaker was half-drunk and all-cook as, uninvited, he sat down at our table, clutching a bottle of beer in his hand.

"Look at you!" he snarled.

Since I knew that I had not looked so lovely since I lost that which I shall soon regain, I gave him a madonna smile and said, "Burger off, Whittaker."

But he was not about to go. He proceeded to make us a drunken speech in which he affected a peculiar Southern accent somewhat like that of the late Lyndon Johnson, whose own performance was a mere shadow of Gene Autry's.

Incidentally, I have just learned that during my five years' absence not only has President Johnson left us but also Jeffrey Hunter, born Henry H. McKinnies, whose memorable starring role in *King of Kings* was the last important Hollywood film—though I have not yet become acquainted with the latest product since Myron has seen almost nothing but TV commercials. Jeff suddenly died in 1969, aged forty-two. How? Why? I had a good cry over that; and suspect foul play.

"Look here, Breckinridge, this is a man's country because no woman can do a burgering thing except break powells, and never will be able to! I know. I had 'em all. Every kind. Every type. Crying for it. Begging for it, they were. Including the libbies from Women's Lib who're really the lesbies. Get it? You got it? Good. Because I got it. And they know I got it. Their number, that is. But you have to hunker down to beat 'em, the way I do. In every department including the kitchen. I can cook any woman's blackmun off, do you hear me, Breckinridge? And stop screwing up your mouth like that. And get out of that drag outfit. Act like a man, Breckinridge, a real man like we all used to be before the powell-cutters got loose and we were turned into a bunch of under-glass capons—at least the few of us who didn't fight it. You got that, Breckinridge? There's still *a few of us* who're fighting to be all-men. To be tough. To kill if we have to. Because that's what it is to be a man, Breckinridge. It's to kill. To stick that breadknife in a woman's whizzer white and make the blood come gushing out! That's what being a man is, Breckinridge. That's what the orgasm is all about. Murder is sex, sex is murder."

I listened to this crazed harangue, delivered in a corn-pone accent picked up in that mess hall of the quarter-master corps where Whittaker spent his war years, frying things in lard for hungry hillbilly boys who are really sweet as lambs except for a tendency, in an offhand way, to beat up lard-blackmuns like Whittaker Kaiser. Then, too, there is nothing so dark or so violent as the soul of a cook. According to police statistics, cooks are responsible for more acts of violence than are the members of any other profession except that of the police themselves.

I dealt coolly with Whittaker; yet ready at a moment's notice to introduce him into the Lotus-in-the-Northwind karate-twist which would fling his fat soft cook's body over my left shoulder and into the jukebox.

"Sex," I said, *ex cathedra,* "is sticking a rehnquist not a knife into a woman's whizzer white."

"You're sick. You're a sick fruit."

"Shut up!" I smiled at Whittaker, preparing for the knockout. "Sex is the union of two things. *Any* two things whether concave or convex or in any combination or number in order to provide more joy for all or any concerned with the one proviso that no little stranger appear as the result of hetero high jinks. So life not death is the big O. Write that down, Whittaker. Tattoo it on your fat blackmun. Drop the news into that frying pan of a brain of yours sizzling with greasy dreams of murder to be served up like McDonald's French fries with real blood for ketchup. A yummy dish for the typical hard-hat soft rehnquistman like you . . ."

With a scream, Whittaker charged me.

I threw the Lotus-in-the-Northwind at him but it misfired. Apparently the Breckinridge reflexes have been slowed down from too much TV-watching in the Valley. Fortunately I was able, easily, to get out of his way. As he crashed into the wall, I picked up my handbag, swung it three times about my head to gain maximum velocity, then connected with Whittaker's head and knocked that tedious chef out cold.

Eddie Mannix and the bartender carried Whittaker from the barroom. The patrons applauded. I smiled shyly my Joan Leslie smile.

But I fear that my victory was spoiled. Half-Cherokee did not come. In fact, he has—according to a blowsy hooker—pulled up stakes and moved permanently to Stockton. I was stunned; broken hearted. Like a Zoë Akins heroïne, I sat there in the lurid light from the jukebox—a dazzling smile upon my lips, a tinkling laugh and a gay word for all; yet in my eyes there was a darkness which only the magic of George Cukor's Brownie could have captured.

How easily broken is a woman's heart! Now I must find another stud.

15

I had it out with Maude this afternoon when he started talking about "our" last-night adventures.

We were in the lobby of the hotel and so had it pretty much to ourselves, for Rooster Van Upp was busy showing to her room a shook-up lady who got into the movie early this morning and can't stop crying. Rooster, I must admit, is very soothing.

"There is something, Maude, I think you better understand about me and that is that I am not who you think I am or was last night." I think I straightened Maude out without going into too much detail, leaving out the surgery bit and just keeping my story to plain old-fashioned schizophrenia, like Dr. Jekyll and Mr. Hyde starring . . . No! Every time I think of an old movie it means that Myra—you whizzer white!—is trying to push her way back up into my head. Well, I'm not playing ball. So forget it.

Of course Maude naturally had to have his little joke about which was Dr. Jekyll and which was Mr. Hyde, since he plainly preferred that drag queen of last night to the company of—I don't deny, am proud of it—a square member of the silent majority who honors the flag and is in Chinese Catering.

"Where by the way does Myra keep her drag out-fit?"

"You'll never know, sweetie. Her wardrobe is my sacred trust."

"What has Myra told you about me?"

"All she said was that sometimes she has these sort of fits and becomes the crashing bore she was when I first met her—no offense, sweetie, I am just quoting and you know how she talks."

"Well, you can tell her from me that if I find that outfit of hers I am going to burn it and meanwhile I am devoting my every waking moment to getting the hell out of here and back to Mary-Ann, my wife, and our analyst who will soon set me straight, maybe with a hormone cocktail."

"Myra's not too eager to go back," said Maude mischievously.

"We'll see," I said, not feeling at all confident about anything.

"In fact, she wants to stay. Why, just yesterday we were looking through the yellow pages together for a plastic surgeon in Culver City who could pop over here and cut off your rehnquist. Such a pity, too! Because I dig what you've got, Myron even if my girl friend doesn't. Anyway, the only plastic surgeon in the book is on vacation at Arrowhead, but when he gets back—*snip!*"

At that moment Rooster Van Upp appeared at the desk, smiling and looking very serious. I got up and said, "Could I talk to you a second, Rooster?"

"Certainly, Mr. Breckinridge."

Rooster and I went into his office, which is a cub-byhole back of the desk with a brand-new old Dumont TV set. "I can't get it to work," said Rooster. "I've tried and tried but all I get is what looks like this blizzard and I know how much you out-of-towners like watching video."

"Rooster, you know what's going on, don't you?" I took the bull by the horns. Rooster never stops smiling his celluloid-teeth smile even though his small red eyes never look at yours and he has a permanent frown. A tricky customer. "Well, Myron, I've heard a few rumors, yes. For instance, I've heard that for three nights running you've been seen at my good friend and colleague Eddie Mannix's bar in women's clothes, raising hell."

I must've turned purple. For some reason Myra's activities never seem to have anything to do with me until somebody says something. "I can explain that," I explained but actually I wasn't about to and he didn't seem to care.

Live and let live is our motto on the Strip. Just play it cool and keep your hands off, say, minors, and your average local Culver City cop will lay off as he is paid to lay off by me among other innkeepers and bonifaces along the Strip." I blushed this time for myself, thinking of sixteen-year-old Chicken's dewy golden armpit.

"It's all a game I—we—Maude—I mean Mr. Trojan and I are playing. To fool the locals, you might say."

"Well, the Mannix Motel is a wide-open establishment and if you think you really want to—uh, keep up this sort of game I think Mr. Eddie Mannix will be happy to let you have one of his cabins."

I could not believe my ears! I am apparently well on my way to being a person non grata at the Irving Thalberg Hotel. Well, it's not my fault. Unfortunately there's no way I can explain that to Rooster so I just changed the subject.

"I have wanted for some time, in fact ever since I got here"—I looked at the Varga girl calendar behind Rooster's desk—"thirteen days ago—to talk to Mr. Williams, but whenever I get him on the phone which is not as often as I'd like and ask him for an interview, he tells me to write my name in that book at the desk, which I've done, and still no answer. I've *got* to see him."

"Well, Myron, I can see that things may be coming

to a head and at our next powwow which will be day after tomorrow I'll tell Mr. Williams that I think it's like urgent for you to sit down and chew the rag with him."

That was the end of that.

Outside the hotel Mrs. Connally Yarborough Bowles gave me a frosty smile. I guess word of Mrya's high jinks has spread.

"There will be a presentation tomorrow, Mr. Breckinridge. A new arrival. I hope you'll attend. In the rumpus room. At nine. A gentleman. From Washington, D.C. The nation's captial."

"Oh, yes, ma'am." I over did the good "Chinese Catering to Your Home" manners. But I need allies in the war with Myra. Not to mention in the coming showdown with Mr. Williams. "I wonder if you could put in a word to Mr. Williams that I would like a word with him."

"Oh, but I haven't seen him in ever so long! Not in a coon's age. In his charming suite. On the second floor. With the reproductions of the old masters. The first editions. And all the sets of beautiful books in their fine Heritage Club bindings. Read, read, read, that's Mr. Williams. From Albany originally. Of an old River family. I will convey your request of course."

This afternoon was to be my afternoon on duty at the Grand Staircase of Babylon set where I was supposed to wait around in case there were any new arrivals.

So I decided to cross over early to the lot and work my way by slow degrees back into the movie. It still takes me time to get used to the *DISSOLVES* and *CUTS* without getting sick.

Just inside the gate who should I see but Whittaker Kaiser with a bandage across his swollen nose and the beginnings of a black eye.

When Whittaker saw me he scowled and automatically crouched down like a overweight chimpanzee and then waddled toward me in a way he thinks is threatening. It was lucky for him I'm not Myra.

"So how's it going, old buddy?" I asked, real nice. Well, Whittaker became very old buddy himself and started grinning in what I guess he thinks is a boyish way and said, "Boy, you sure pack some wallop, Myron. You really laid one on me in the bar. The doc says my nose is fractured."

"Sorry about that, Whittaker, but . . ."

"Hell, Myron. Let's let bygones be bygones."

I was relieved that he had dropped the Lyndon Johnson cornpone talk and now sounded sort of breathy and nervous and solemn like Richard M. Nixon our President when he's really got something difficult to explain to us on the TV and knows that he is surrounded by enemies who will later try to distort his every word in the interest of an alien philosophy.

"I guess I was drinking pretty heavy in the bar last night and then of course I always see red—now don't get mad—when I see a guy carrying on like a woman when it's bad enough for a woman to be carrying on like a woman. No offense intended," he added quickly, afraid of Myra's quick repartee and knee to the groin.

"Well, Whittaker, what can I say? It just so happens that I see myself as your average John Q. Citizen who's kind of a bluenose about these things."

"That wasn't the way you were acting in the bar."

"Well, I have this . . . uh, comedy routine I do. Sort of like Milton Berle, remember? On the TV? In the lady's hat?" I improvised fast and not too well. So far I have no defenses against the inroads Myra is making on my reputation not to mention on my mind where she is fighting for control at this very minute and will break through one of these days once and for all if I don't get some hormones soon along with friendly counsel from the family analyst. I am certain it is basically a matter of diet. I have noticed that there is altogether too much refined sugar being eaten here in the forties and un-enriched bread.

"Look, Myron, I got great respect for you." Beware of a cook bearing grease! "I can tell we got a lot in common. We both want to get out of here. That's the most important thing. And of course I've got these crazy drives, too. Who hasn't? I mean what red-blooded all-male-man hasn't got these urges? But, Myron, you got to fight those other impulses. Of course women are keating. Of course sex with women is a steaming, sickening mess, but God damn it, Myron, the real man goes through with it! And if he can't get it up because the woman is loathsome, he's got to keep trying, front, back, sideways. *Somehow* he's got to do it because that's what makes him a man! Even if he has to take a knife to her to get it up, he's got to or he won't be a man but a fag who has given up, surrendered, taken himself out of the only game there is, getting women away from other men—from other women, too—and at the risk of losing his sanity sometimes, he's got to plow deep into that swamp, that awful sickening place . . ."

Whittaker was very worked up. Also, I noticed that he had started pronouncing swamp "swaw-yump" which meant he was going overboard again and into his Lyndon Johnson hillbilly Genghis Khan number and I would soon be forced to continue the work that Myra has begun and really break his nose.

But Mr. Telemachus and Iris—of all people—came strolling toward us and I shouted "Hi," and they started to come over and I said, "Whittaker, if you hate women so much, why don't you leave them alone? Get yourself a boy or something."

"I explained it. You weren't listening." Whittaker was getting very white around the mouth. "I guess it's the way I use language that is difficult for some people with no attention span to dig. Look, every man wants to make it with another man but the *real* man is the one who fights this hideous weak fag self and takes one woman after another without the use of any contraceptives or pill or diaphragm or rubber, just the all-conquering sperm because contraception of any kind if as bad as masturbation and because the good burger makes the good baby . . ."

And so on for a reprise which didn't end until Mr. Telemachus and Iris joined us.

Whittaker gives me the creeps. But I think Iris likes him and for her sake I hope he stays away from the old kitchen knife in the coming days. I introduced them all around, and then proceeded on my way alone into the picture and my lookout station at Shot 128.

Along the way, feeling sort of tired, I sat down behind a lilac bush in front of a Chinese pagoda left over from *The Good Earth* and got a load off my feet. Since it's a real nice day, I just sat awhile, not even making any notes in this book. So while I was just sitting there, suddenly I saw coming toward me these two men who were dragging this third man between them. One of the two men was the big hulk I saw my first day, Luke. The other was a dapper-looking Negro in a white suit and wearing a white Panama hat. The men they were kind of holding up and dragging between them was wearing one of those rubber Richard M. Nixon masks that you can buy in the novelty shops and are in such bad taste.

The three men didn't see me as they walked past the Chinese pagoda. I was just about to say "Hi," but thank God, I didn't or I would not be almost home as I am now.

What stopped me from saying "Hi" was the man with the rubber mask who was saying in a funny quavery kind of voice, "Actually, there's no . . . uh, hurry. I mean I thought I might look around for a place to stay. Nothing fancy. Of course, I'll need your latest electronic equipment. That's in the interest of national security. As is your best authentic redwood wind screen, and some of those ornamental shrubberies, and one of your jumbo-size electric ice crushers. Also a ceramic tile shuffleboard. That's a must."

The Negro was very polite and sounded just like a white man when he said, "I'm afraid, sir, that won't be possible."

Well, when he said that the man in the rubber mask sort of struggled a bit but the Negro and Luke had a good grip on him and just as they passed me and I was about to step forward the Negro said, "We're sending you home, sir. It's our duty. It's *your* duty."

"No. No. Going home, that would be the easy way. That would be a cop-out."

Home! *Boing.* This light went on in my head. *They were on their way to the exit to send this man home!* Well, I sneaked along behind them, hiding behind bushes and trees, overhearing some but not all of their conversation.

The man in the mask sounded very upset at having to leave. "I mean I'd hoped for a longer visit. Like . . . uh, five years. Statute of limitations. We had this checked out very carefully. It was my responsibility, let me say right off. To keep the cap on the bottle. First I sent Claypoole of the FBI . . ."

The Negro said, "We have our quota, sir, and Mr. Claypoole is it. Or will be it when he arrives on schedule. As for yourself, feel free to apply again in a few years . . ."

"That will be too late. At least let me take this burgering mask off."

The Negro looked at Luke, who said, "We're past the point where the locals can see us."

"You may remove the mask, sir."

Well, I guess you could've knocked me over with a feather because under that rubber Richard M. Nixon mask was Richard M. Nixon, wearing heavy makeup and sweating like he had been in a turkish bath. Now let me make one thing absolutely clear. I don't rule out conspiracy and that this *might* have been a double except that no double could sweat like our President or *sound* that much like him when he's sweating.

I'm afraid I didn't listen to what our President was

saying as carefully as I ought to have because I was waiting for one of the other two to say something about where the exit is, which Luke did which is why I am here, waiting for them because I ran as fast as I could in order to get here first which wasn't hard since they are walking very slowly and every now and then Mr. Nixon wants to sit down and rest.

But some of what I heard went like this. "Spiro . . . Mr. Agnew, the Vice-President and one of the finest men I have ever met in public life." Amen to that, I said to myself. "When you look him in the eye, you know he's got it . . ."

"True, true," said the Negro in a snotty way.

"Spiro would take over. We would have this announcement. Something simple. Saying that for reasons of . . . uh, health, I have gone back to this year, to 1948 . . . one of the best years, let me say, in the best country in the history of this nation, and I have taken up residence inside *Siren of Babylon*—a really great film, which is also great entertainment *for the whole family*. What else? I mean I certainly would not want to *see* much less *live* inside of an X-rated movie *because it would be wrong*. That's for sure."

"True, Mr. President. But I fear that in this hour of peril your country needs you. Watergate needs you . . ."

"How does a million dollars grab you? It would be wrong but . . ." Well, the President went on and on like that, making absolutely no sense to me. I suppose that he was like always being devil's advocate which means you try to give both sides of a knotty moral issue in order to find out what the right thing to do is.

Then Luke said something about the exit being just opposite the Grand Staircase and that they'd better hurry up and that's when I sprinted off just as Mr. Nixon was, as usual, examining carefully all his options by asking, "Is there an extradition treaty between 1948 and the future?"

I am now sitting near where the exit is soon going to be. Just now I saw the three of them on the other side of the set. Mr. Nixon seems to be putting up some kind of struggle which I don't quite understand as he has so many good things going for him back in the White House. Well, in a minute he and I are going through that gate . . .

16

It was touch and go for an instant. Five minutes before Mr. Nixon was shoved screaming through the exit, I took possession of the Breckinridge psyche, preventing Myron from getting even so much as a glimpse of where the exit is and how it is made to open.

There *was* an awkward moment when the dinge and the mountain of gristle known as Luke saw me a few scenes later, but I put on one of Myron's truly cretinous expressions and said that I had just arrived in the film and was waiting to take up my post at Shot 128. Convinced that I had seen nothing untoward, they hurried out of the film.

But let us forget the trivial Mr. Nixon, who will, in any case, never be elected President as a result of what I am now doing! Let us contemplate the truly important.

Siren of Babylon!

17

The joy of actually being inside the film of *Siren of Babylon* is beyond description!

Right off, I could hardly believe that there, only a few yards away from me, was Bruce Cabot—handsome, virile, masterful if a bit paunchy, for he is now forty-four years old and fifteen years of good living have passed since Bruce was the glorious pith-helmeted youth of *King Kong* fame (1933).

As I watched Bruce swirling his cape at the foot of the Grand Staircase, waiting for Maria Montez to descend, I found it almost unbearable to think that two years ago (1971) he died, and even worse, that this handsome if somewhat corpulent swashbuckling romantic star of Mexican extraction who gave me such delight for many an afternoon (no, for an entire lifetime!) will in almost no time at all become the bloated character actor in Sam Spiegel's *The Chase* (1966), a film whose only distinction was the hair-styling of the late Miriam Hopkins.

I almost screamed when I got my first glimpse of Maria on the Grand Staircase. It is so different actually being inside the picture! So much more vivid, more real— even though one can see that the actors are sweating under their heavy makeup and that the sets are just painted canvas. Also, I am able to see the technicians beyond the set. Yet no matter how hard I try, I cannot see the camera which is seeing us or the director behind the camera or anything, in fact, past the frame of the action except a blue-gray void.

Experimentally I moved toward the void—careful to avoid the exit.

At a certain point I discovered—nothing. As usual, I have found the right word. One feels nothing; one sees nothing; one simply stops. It is the end of wherever we are but *my* beginning because I could happily spend eternity examining just this one film, frame by frame, reveling in the dialogue, the lighting, the makeup.

Most delicious of all, I am able to study the actors in close detail during the commercial and station breaks when the action stops and the actors freeze.

One of the interesting ground rules: if you stand just past the frame of the action on the side where the camera ought to be, you are in the quotidian. That is, the movie is being made right then and there, with all the takes and various hazards of union overtime. But if you step into the frame of the film from the opposite side, you are, literally, *in the picture,* exactly as it is shown on television with all the station and commercial breaks. This is known as "breaking frame" on the Strip. One of the taboos that I have now shattered.

Since some of the commercials go on selling cars for ten minutes at a time, I am able to circulate on the set and actually touch the players. Yes, it is possible to *feel* the characters in *Siren of Babylon* even though the stars are dead and I am sure that half the extras must be dead, too, or in the old actors' home.

Creepy but exciting to be able to go up to Maria Montez—how tall she is!—with her glamorous makeup and golden crown, and pass one's hand in front of her obsidian black eyes and see no response in them save a reflection of one's own hand, as though it had been for an instant engraved upon some dark negative of the soul.

Does her mind unconsciously retain a picture of me on her retina? Inhaling her divine aroma (perfume with a gardenia base) and feeling, let me confess, with hungry curiosity, her beautiful father hills beneath the gilded breastplate she wears in the banquet scene. Let me note for posterity that her father hills, though fine, did not in life approach in magnificence those that I have lost but will one day regain.

Maria *must* see me, and if she sees me she must remember me. But of course she cannot retain much memory because for her on a June day in 1948 all this is *continuous* action while for me (in 1973 *and* in 1948) the action has been frozen by the Used Car Dealers Association of Van Nuys. What is five minutes eight seconds for me is a meson of time for her: a brief shadow across the face, a mote in the klieg lights.

When the action starts again, I am *pulled* from the frame of action. No other verb will do. Since this "pull" is not a powerful force, I suspect it comes from inside oneself and not from, say, the director of the film or from the management of Loew's Incorporated which pulls *all* strings at Culver City under the able leadership of company president Nicholas M. Schenck in New York.

Almost delirious with joy, I went through the film not once but twice. I even enjoyed the buffeting one gets during the *CREDITS*! This is Hollywood! This is magic!

I had also never realized what a splendid actress Maria Montez was. "Oh, foul King Nebuchadnezzar," she says with spitfire intensity to Louis Calhern, who plays that ill-starred monarch just before the writing on the wall appears, the work of a special-effects man from Disney.

"You who have debauched thousands and listened to evil councillors, now will you listen to the voice of the One True God?"

Every time Maria says this line I shiver and want to pee and am covered with gooseflesh. Her air of Puerto Rican majesty combined with a Santo Domingan accent result in a performance which is, voice-wise, superior to that of Loretta Young as Berengaria in *The Crusaders* (1935) when Loretta said so movingly to her husband

Richard the Lion-Hearted, "Richard, you gotta save Christianity," and equal to that of Lana Turner's portrayal of a priestess of Ba'al who is stoned to death in *The Prodigal* (1955): a performance which was, very simply, the high point of 1940's movie acting in a 1950's film.

Luckily no one joined us from outside the movie or I would have proved to be poor Virgil to any TV-watching Dante as I allowed myself to be hurled deliriously from scene to scene, over and over again, learning by heart the dialogue, detecting new glories in the décor, getting to know not only the stars intimately but the extras as well.

Yes, *extras!* I am not a snob. Far from it. As I moved among the Babylonian army during the commercials, I lifted a good many of the skirts the soldiers wear (designed by Travis Banton) and delighted in the variety of anachronistic undergarments—dance belts, Jockey shorts, white World War II navy drawers with the name of the owner stenciled in black across the seat, olive-drab army shorts, jockstraps.

Needless to say, I amused myself by going to the root of each young man's—not to mention the world's—problem. In the process, I discovered to my amazement and horror that two thirds are circumcised. This is a great blow for me, for these young men costumed as Babylonian soldiers are the very same young men who only three years earlier as American soldiers, sailors and marines defeated the Axis powers, and it was always my understanding that the youths of that heroic era had *not* been criminally mutilated by the surgeon's knife and so, foreskins intact, they had been able to conquer the world. Now I must revise my notes on the golden age or do more work in the field.

I do not rule out the possibility that those young men who are destined to be movie extras must suffer mutilation not only psychically—that goes without saying—but *physically* in order to make them amenable to direction without billing and so members in good standing of the Screen Extras Guild. This could be a major insight and the *donnée* of an important essay for *Films and Filming* now that the *Cahiers du Cinéma* is strictly Stalinist. Certainly I am in an amazing position, able to report on the genitals of several hundred extras in an MGM film of 1948. It is like being present at the siege of Troy. I also cannot help but think how different the world would be if I could *remove* all those superfluous tubes and knobs! As it is, in twenty-five years time these three hundred-odd male extras will have contributed 2.3 children apiece to our burgeoning population. In turn these 690 new citizens will produce 1,597 by the year . . . Monstrous, monstrous nature! It was all I could do not to start hacking away then and there.

Quite by accident I discovered that it is possible to alter *Siren of Babylon*. In the scene where Maria Montez summons four soldiers to her presence and gives them orders to kill Bruce Cabot (there has been a rift between the lovers), I was very taken with one of the soldiers, a tall youth of perhaps twenty with bright red hair hidden beneath a Babylonian helmet and swarthy makeup. I was not aware of his true coloring until I lifted up his skirt and with a now practiced hand scooped my hand inside the sweaty jockstrap and let fall free as fine a set of boyish baubles as ever adorned a member of the Screen Extras Guild—a snow-white rehnquist decorated with the most delicate blue veins and, best of all, heroic! That is, uncircumcised. The added glory of bright gold-red pubic hair so entranced me (against my better judgment, let me say: although I am aware of the lethal nature of these machines I am also, let me confess, a mere woman, susceptible to atavistic impulses old as the race) that I lingered too long. As the off-camera pull began, I hastily relinquished my grip on the redhead's rehnquist and the skirt fell back into place . . . almost.

Two hours later when I had returned to the same scene, I noticed that *the skirt did not fall free:* the elastic of the jockstrap had caught the material of the costume, baring two inches of white unpainted and definitely un-Babylonian thigh. The fact that the audience's attention is entirely on Maria at this moment means that only a few film buffs will ever note the slightly unkempt look of one of the Babylonian soldiers.

The possibilities, however, of *intervention* are fascinating. But are they limitless? Presumably the editor of the film will catch any important changes that I make. Yet he is long since dead or retired as of now (1973). It is all very puzzling. I am both now and then. The makers of the film are entirely then. Presumably what they made *then* cannot be altered *now*, yet I have slightly changed one scene, and for at least one showing on television in the San Fernando Valley area my alteration was detectable. Somewhat alarmed at the possibilities, I decided to undo what I had done the next time I came to the scene.

I also decided to play a little trick on the red-haired extra. I took from my pocket one of a half dozen Chinese fortunes which that schmuck Myron is in the habit of stuffing into cookies for the delight of his rustic clients. This one said "You will meet your one true love."

On the back of the thin rice paper I wrote "Mannix Motel Bar Saturday June 30 9:00 P.M. love Myra." During the station break I hurried onto the set, lifted the soldier's skirt and took in my hand the long rehnquist which still hung rather uncomfortably outside the right jockstrap (he is suffering, I noted, either from prickly heat or jock itch—strawberry blotches in the hot rosy crotch). Deftly I pulled back the loose foreskin to reveal a shiny mauve-tinted rehn. I then wrapped the Chinese fortune around the neck of the quist and restored the foreskin to its usual protective position. As I scooped the whole floppy apparatus back into the jockstrap, I yanked hard at one of the red curls that sprang out on either side of the tight elastic. The curl came free: a souvenir! I straightened the boy's skirt and withdrew from the scene.

One reel later Mr. Telemachus arrived to take my place at the Great Staircase scene. "Anybody come through?"

"No," I said, playing it like Myron. "It's been real quiet."

We chatted for a few scenes. Mr. Telemachus told me

that he never watches the movie any more. "I know it by heart."

"But there is so much to see. To learn."

"Glad you're getting with it. You should. You're new. I used to be the same. Now it bores the keating out of me. But then, I'm in the Industry."

I confess that anyone who has ever worked for *Daily Variety* excites me, and Mr. Telemachus was no exception.

We talked of various matters during the army mutiny scene in which my redhead distinguishes himself—unaware that twenty-five years later Myra Breckinridge, battered but unbowed, not only has sent him a message in a most provocative way ("meet cute" is the first law of the classic Hollywood film and I am proud to say that I have not transgressed this primal commandment), but next Saturday will initiate him into delights undreamed of since Pasiphaë surrendered to Minos the holy maze king.

While chatting of this and that, my unconscious mind was at work restructuring the universe—starting with Red. Looking at him, I suddenly realized that with the telephone lineman I had been barking up the wrong tree. True, Half-Cherokee would have made a perfect Indian princess but there would also have been, I realized suddenly, innumerable *ethnic* demonstrations as well as unjust charges of genocide aimed at the original American. Anyway, Half-Cherokee has skipped town.

Watching Red, I *knew* that I had stumbled upon the perfect subject. With a bit of work, Red would make a totally luscious Amazon on the order of Rhonda Fleming, currently (1948) lensing *A Connecticut Yankee in King Arthur's Court*. In fact, if Red's vocal quality is sufficiently nasal, there is no reason why he could not take over some of the roles that Rhonda, more interested in domesticity than filming, turned down during the fifties, depriving the world audience of the only bona-fide Amazonian redhead since the advent of color.

"You still want to go back, Myron?"

"Well, I don't know." I played it like Myron. *Go back!*

I would rather go direct to the Forest Lawn Slumber Room than ever again live as Myron in the Valley! Wild producers could not drag me from the Strip, from *Siren of Babylon*!

I am where I want to be, and of how many people can this be said? The only thing that stands in my way is Myron (and *his* thing) but I do not for an instant doubt that I will win this battle as I have won all the others in my quest for uniqueness. I am a self-creation both perfect and complete. Yet, paradoxically, protean and still evolving toward . . . Not even I know *exactly* what but I suspect. The enormity of the role that I am now required to play humbles, exalts me.

"Because, Myron, what we've got here is a fine way of life, as everyone who has come onto the Strip agrees."

"I've got a real nice way of life back home." I played the part of a homesick Chinese caterer to the hilt.

"I don't think there's much chance of any of us getting out anyway."

"I guess not," I said, sounding sad. To my knowledge there has never been a movie star more convincing than Myra Breckinridge when it comes to acting both behavioral and technical. Certainly my work is superior to that of Joanne Woodward whose performance in *The Three Faces of Eve* is but the palest carbon of my own story. Yet for the Dixie Duse's mild exertions in Nunnally Johnson's film, *she* was given the Oscar! On that downward sliding scale, I deserve at the very least the Nobel Peace Prize!

"If there was a way out Mr. Williams would've found it," said Mr. Telemachus.

"How could he if he spends all his time in his suite, reading *books*?"

"Not all the time. According to the grapevine he often holds confabs on the blower with Louis B. Mayer."

"Then it *is* possible for us to ring the front office?"

"Why not? But will they call back? That's where the heartache comes in show biz."

"They will call *me* back, Mr. Telemachus."

On this powerful note, I left the film, enjoying to the fullest the last slow buffeting in the *CREDITS*.

It was growing dark as I walked on air down Andy Hardy's street—so lovely and folksy and American in the gloaming. Fireflies hovering in the rosebushes. I could almost smell the apple pie Fay (Mom Hardy) Holden is baking for our boy.

Just as I got to the Strip, I felt faint as Myron made a desperate effort to seize control, hoping that I had been weakened by the *CREDITS,* but I am made of stronger stuff than any mere caterer. I hurled him to the bottom of our mutual well. Now—full speed ahead! Operation Myra: Phase Two!

With a heart full of gladness for all mankind, including Red, for whom I have my little plans, I went straight from the Thalberg Hotel to my hideaway cabin at the Mannix, collecting Maude on the way.

Maude was, I fear, down in the dumps.

"Do you realize, sweetie, that here it is 1973 and I still don't know what Mr. Kenneth is doing? I haven't had any real word since that girl from Vidal Sassoon's hair-bending parlor in New York arrived two years ago. I'm cut off from the world!"

"Don't fret, Maude. Think of all you have going for you in this marvelous place."

"Oh, I'm not ungrateful. It's just that it seems very strange that for two years absolutely no one who knows anything about hair has come through, that's all."

During this, I was putting on my clothes, transforming myself from drab Chinese caterer to glittering Myra Breckinridge, the siren of 1948, a year whose fashions fit me to a T (like all the other important stars I ignore the New Look and its hideous leg-hiding skirts).

Even Maude was forced to admit that given the sleaziness of the materials he has rustled up for me, the ultimate effect was stunning, particularly with a drop or two of belladonna in each eye to give me that gleaming vulnerable little-girl-lost look so reminiscent of poor Gail Russell. "I've known many a drag queen in my day, sweetie, but you're the tops."

I could not let that low blow go unparried. "Maude," I said, achieving that very special vocal quality which has been known to make the marrow of the cockiest stud turn to water. "I am not a drag queen. Repeat: I am not that most ridiculous of creatures. I am Myra Breckinridge. Admittedly damaged, mutilated but, Maude, *unbowed!* The anomaly, the imposter, the travesty is *Myron* Breckinridge."

I think Maude got the point.

As we crossed to the bar for our evening apéritif, I saw an open convertible slowly passing by, apparently headed for the Texaco station. In it were two young men. Note how calmly, how simply I record this information. It is as if St. Paul were to start telling *his* tall tale with the casual remark that "while making good time one morning on the road to Damascus, I happened to see this funny-looking specimen standing on the side of the road —a hitchhiker, I thought."

Well, those two young men in that open convertible were none other than William Eythe and Lon ("Bud") McCallister. I confess that when I recognized them, I screamed.

They looked around; and beneath the feigned alarm on their legendary faces, I could detect admiration, yes, even *lust* as their eyes focused on me.

But then I am afraid that I started to *run* after their car. Yes, I lost my head! I kept calling out their names and this I fear was simply not cool of me, for they did not, after all, stop at the Texaco station. In fact, William gunned the motor of his "wheels" as they used to call their jalopies back in those—these days and in a cloud of exhaust they were gone.

Maude was much amazed. "Sweetie, you've got to get used to movie stars. They drive along here all the time."

"But . . . but . . ." That was the extent of my eloquence. For once I was silenced by emotion. How could I ever express to this Paganini of hair—to anyone—what it is that I feel about those two mythic youths now seen by me in the actual flesh at the height of their glory and *in the round*—an effect so far not truly possible in the movies despite various attempts like *House of Wax*, where one was obliged to hold up cardboard spectacles containing red and green celluloid in order to get a sense of the third dimension whose absence—and one must face this fact squarely—has *made* the art of cinema unique and glorious, for in its very flatness celluloid is as complete and final as the walls of the Sistine Chapel or of the Radio City Music Hall. Yes, as two-dimensional and triumphantly flat as a page of the *Divine Comedy*. To give either the movies or the pages of a classic actual depth would be to mar perfection, to make confusion where all is now clarity. Yet, I confess, that for me to see *in person* movie stars of yesteryear *in* yesteryear is something else again, and creates euphoria.

Like Carole Landis, William Eythe had no back to his head; each died young. He of a liver complaint; she a suicide. But Lon ("Bud") McCallister lives on, I am told, doing well with his many business enterprises in and around Malibu, and though one is happy for him today (1973), he is of course no longer the boy who broke your heart in *Stage Door Canteen*, playing Romeo to Katharine Cornell's gracious Juliet nor can he ever again go home, except on the Late Show, to Indiana.

What a beautiful couple they were this afternoon! But William will soon be dead, still a boy. My eyes are full of tears (not to mention Maude's vile belladonna) as I write these lines in my cabin at the Mannix Motel, where I have moved officially and with the blessing of Mr. Williams, whom I spoke to on the telephone earlier this evening.

Mr. Williams was polite. I was polite, and firm. "I believe, Mr. Williams, that all things considered, it is best for me to transfer myself to the Mannix Motel where I find an atmosphere more to my taste, more congenial in every way."

I gave Mr. Mannix a wink (we were in his office) and

he seemed pleased despite a face as expressionless as that of Virginia O'Brien, though hardly as cute. Incidentally, I think Metro never used Virginia correctly. But then even without hindsight it is plain to me that Hollywood is responding to television in the wrong manner. Instead of increasing the "pure" Hollywood product, Dore Schary is trying perversely to "upgrade" the product, poor bastard, because when the day of reckoning comes eight years from now (1956) he will be out on his blackmun and MGM—which is Hollywood—will go into permanent eclipse.

Fortunately my master plan requires that *I* take over the company. Knowing what I know of past films plus what I know of the disasters in preparation at this very moment (1948), I have every confidence that I can, with the cooperation of the various guilds and unions and of those organizations and individuals who have made the Industry great, continue the golden age of Hollywood for another decade, and perhaps indefinitely. Who knows?

Mr. Williams knows. Or suspects. "Of course, Mr. Breckinridge, if you are happier at the motel . . ."

"Please," I interrupted, all darkness and sweet. "Not *Mr.* Breckinridge, *please*. Call me Myra, and I'll call *you* Mr. Williams!"

There was a sound of coughing at the other end. "Of course—Myra. Did you enjoy your first day on duty in the film?"

I could tell that the dinge and Luke had reported to him that I *might* have observed them giving Tricky Dick the old heave-ho but I played it more gelid than usual.

"More than I can say!" Roz Russell could not have played the scene more briskly or with greater sincerity.

"I'm pleased that you are no longer—uh, restless here in our little family."

"Quite the contrary."

"I must remind you, however, Mister—I mean Myra—of that essential rule which we are all obliged to observe for the privilege . . . and I think we agree that it *is* a privilege to be here?"

"Oh, yes!"

"Which is: *never* interfere with the locals."

"But surely, Mr. Williams, carefree friendships of the casual sort . . ."

"Naturally, naturally, one is not a prude. Of course. No, I meant we must never, never *change* anything. On the Strip or on the set."

Was I observed? Does he know? Obviously I must be more careful. "I certainly understand the ground rules. But then, how could we change anything when the locals can't understand us whenever we talk about the future?"

"One can never be certain how much they pick up from us." Oh, he was smooth! It's plain to me that he and Rooster are in cahoots. After all, how could Mr. Williams have made that killing on the stock market using *future* knowledge if he had not been able to communicate with Rooster, or with a broker at the very least? But in the interest of my threefold master plan I was willing to "play dumb," as they say, and on a genial note we signed off.

First and foremost, I must destroy Myron. As soon as that plastic surgeon returns from Arrowhead, I shall remove Mary-Ann's grotesque pacifier and have my *poitrine* restored. Meanwhile, I have put an order in at a nearby pharmacy for the ingredients necessary for the making of a hormone cocktail.

Once Myron is eliminated I shall, gradually, insert myself not only into *Siren of Babylon* (where certain plot changes are absolutely necessary) but into the higher councils of MGM itself. I realize that this will not be easy. After all, there is no way for us of getting from the back lot to the administration building or to the sound stages, but there is still the telephone, and of course the directors, actors, executives can always come here to the Mannix Motel, to confer with their—and I use, as always, the right word—*savior*, for I—and I alone—have been chosen to save Hollywood at this crucial moment when television is about to steal some ninety million worshippers from the gorgeous temples of Loew's, of Paramount, of RKO and of Pantages.

Finally, I shall reduce the population of the world by the sexual transformation of Red. Properly presented by the media, I know that I can make the sterile fun-loving Amazon the ideal identity for every red-blooded American boy. Naturally, I realize that a few boys will object to transformation but I am sure that the American Mom will join with me in "persuading" those oddballs to conform. Meanwhile, sperm banks will be set up in every community and pre-transformation boys will be obliged to make monthly deposits in order that non-sterile Amazons (*born* women, that is) may be inseminated artificially *but rarely* because population in the United States must be reduced by two thirds before the new century begins—my century. Century? How modest I am! Myra's *millennium* is about to dawn.

Sitting with Maude in the Mannix bar, I noticed several keen-looking men with crewcuts, all drinking beer in a quiet boisterous way. Maude said, with a sniff (Maude is the total snob), "They're *technicians*, sweetie, working on *Siren of Babylon.* They're in most every evening. So square. They go home to their wives."

I was intrigued. "Do many people from the picture drop in?"

"Oh, my, yes! During the lunch break we get quite a few."

"Maria? Bruce? Louis?"

"Not the *stars* of the movie, silly! Though Maria did come here once." Maude frowned. "But just for a minute. She was very strange. She knew all about *me,* of course." Maude is such a liar that I discounted this story automatically. "But the grips! We're big as can be on grips and cameramen and extras. Oh, and John Wayne did come in one night with a bunch of cronies and someone at the bar over there, someone drunk, said, 'Hi, Marion!' " Maude giggled. "I nearly fell out of my chair, sweetie. I mean I never *knew!* John Wayne, so butch!"

I was severe. "It just happens, Maude, that John Wayne's real name is *Marion* Michael Morrison."

Maude looked disappointed. "Then I guess I missed

the point. Anyway, there was a row because the drunk was a war veteran who said, 'Tell us, Marion, why, when we was having our blackmuns shot off in the Pacific, you was making *Flying Tigers* in good old Hollywood and never lifted a finger for your Uncle Sam?' "

"That was cruel," I said, trying to be fair. "But we must take the long view. By arranging so wisely to stay out of the Second World War, John Wayne was able to make not only *Flying Tigers* but *They Were Expendable* and those two pictures did more to defeat Tojo than all of General Chennault's air raids on the enemy."

"I hadn't thought of it like that, Myra." There was awe in Maude's voice.

"Of course you hadn't—sweetie." But I was benign. Maude will be a useful accomplice in the exciting days ahead.

Above the rickety table on which I write these notes hangs a calendar. It is Thursday. Will Red come here on Saturday? I am certain that he will if the day on which he was working in that scene with Maria Montez *precedes* this coming Saturday. But it could easily have been shot *after* this Saturday, in which case I shall have to keep a lookout every Saturday until the picture ends. Of course, he might be frightened when he reads the message. Or he might simply wash it away without bothering to look. Or, somber prospect, not wash at all. But, no, he was clean if sweaty. He will come Saturday and through him I will work my way not only into the film but into the decision-making process of Loew's Inc. That is a solemn vow.

In the weak lamplight the gold-red curl gleams on the palm of my hand. What surprises are in store for him!

Locked in my bureau drawer is silicone. A scalpel. Lysol.

18

All right, Myra, so you got back into the driver's seat just as I was heading for the exit with our President, but don't think you'll be able to stop me next time now that I know that (a) there is a way out of here and (b) I know more or less where that particular exit is through which our President, I guess, went as he is no longer here—and I don't dare let on to anybody that I ever saw him as Luke and his Negro friend will then try to keep me away from the exit—which just doesn't make any sense. I mean here I am being forced to stay here where I don't want to be while our President who wanted to take a much-needed vacation in this neck of the woods was made to go back to the White House. Anyway, as far as I can tell, nobody here knows about Mr. Nixon's brief visit except for the Negro, Luke, me and Myra. Now for some very shocking news.

We met in the rumpus room as per usual at nine o'clock. Maude avoids me whenever I am myself. "Oh, you're in one of *those* moods, are you?" He says, "Well, you'll never find Myra's drag. Never!"

Although I wore a sort of raunchy cowboy outfit I bought last week and was careful to walk like some kind of bear with arthritis to show how deeply and sincerely butch I am, I am afraid a snigger was heard from several people among them Chicken Van Upp who blushed bright red when I looked at him hard and tough. At least Myra has scared the boy-element among the locals.

Myra has also pretty much ruined me, if not herself, with the other out-of-towners. I have no idea how they take to her when she is all dressed up. I suppose she compels attention like always. I sure Lord God don't.

Anyway, I sat in the front row at the end with Whittaker Kaiser next to me—the other skunk nobody wants to sit near. "You look good, Myron," he said in his thick cook's voice. "You're fighting this thing."

"Yeah," I said, dropping my voice a couple registers. "I'm trying to beat it once and for all."

"Just remember you got to be absolutely ruthless because that's what kills them, finally, the whizzer whites that are cutting our powells off."

"Amen," I said, meaning it, too. That is just what I am going through now in a way that that dumb cook could never understand.

Mrs. Connolly Yarborough Bowles read the minutes of the last meeting and then introduced "The latest member of our little group—arrival date May 9, 1973—with some very interesting, nay, absolutely crucial news about our country and its institutions. I think we should all. Rise to our feet. As a recognition of the achievements. Of our newest member. J. D. Claypoole. Of the Federal Bureau of Investigation. At Washington, D.C. Until his *removal*. In the weeks following the resignation. Of the acting chief. Of the FBI. Mr. Grey. A former naval person. And resident. Of Connecticut . . ." Mrs. C. Y. Bowles went on adding details like always while we were all very nervous wondering just what the latest news of the Watergate was. I was also extra nervous even shook up because the President had said very clearly that he had personally sent Mr. Claypoole here some time ago and the Negro had said no, that he wasn't here yet like he the Negro knew that Mr. Claypoole was on his way. Well, how did he know this? Are these people *all* Communists?

J. D. Claypoole is about thirty and has a crewcut and wears steel-rimmed spectacles and in his lapel there is a large American flag. Obviously he's doing his best to *seem* like a loyal American. Yet he could very well be a Communist agent in disguise coming back to 1948 to sell America short by betraying our President, which is a very real possibility in the light of the story he had to tell whose highlights as of yesterday are that a number of the President's closest advisers have resigned for having tried to cover up the alleged misdeeds of certain "plumbers" I think was the word he used for those crooks who broke into the Democratic headquarters at the Watergate which is a building in Washington, D.C., and were caught. *Allegedly* they were working for the President in order to reelect him by a large majority, which seems peculiar right off since I don't know anybody our side of Van Nuys in the Valley who was not a Nixon man all the way in that period or frame of time.

We were all pretty stunned—even shook up by the presentation. *Allegedly* our President told the CIA to go and get the psychiatric records of someone named Daniel Burgsell who stole the Pentagon Papers, a story I did not follow too closely as it was not written about very much in our local papers or played up on the local TV station's evening news wrap-ups.

Then there is this adviser to the President, Dean Rusk, who has been in government service for some time I seem to recall who is afraid he will be killed by the President's friends when he tells the true story of how they were all in it either to the Senate Committee or to the television jury whichever comes first.

J. D. Claypoole summed up powerfully: "Ladies and gentlemen, I make you one promise. The Federal

Bureau of Investigation, *your* Federal Bureau of Investigation, is not going to be a setup for this one. When Mr. Nixon went to the Director—and you know who I mean." All over the room the name of "J. Edgar Hoover" was said with a real reverence. "The President said, 'I want you to tap the phones of my staff and the newspapermen they are giving secrets to.' 'Well,' the Director said, 'this is not in my line of work but I will do as you order as you are the President if you put your request in writing signed by the Attorney General,' and Mr. Nixon did and then when he came under the influence of the Communist conspiracy, shortly after his notorious trips to Peking and Moscow . . ."

I tell you we were all reeling in the rumpus room, at least those of us who are good Americans and hit the Strip post-1968 and voted for Nixon. Because to tell the truth a lot of folks in the Valley were stunned, yes, shook up when our President visited the two centers of the monolithic Communist world conspiracy.

Now here is J. D. Claypoole, a true-blue FBI investigator and loyal sidekick to the great Director himself, telling us that "Mr. Nixon tried to force the Director to resign to implement further the plans drawn up for Mr. Nixon in Moscow and Peking and that is why the Director said, 'If you try to force me out, I will publish your order to me to wiretap illegally your own staff and certain members of the fourth estate.' Well, that was the end of that, ladies and gentlemen. The Director died in harness, the way he would've wanted it. But once he was out of the way Mr. Nixon, acting on orders from his masters in Moscow and Peking, replaced him with a malleable tool. That is why the republic is in danger of total collapse tonight or should I say twenty-five years, give or take a month or two, from tonight."

There was a fierce hubbub at this point with everybody asking questions which didn't really stop until Maude asked the usual question about hair-styling and what was Mr. Kenneth up to and J. D. Claypoole made a very funny if sort of cruel take-off of poor Maude by lisping, while patting his crewcut, "Call me Goldilocks!" The meeting broke up on this very humorous note.

Whittaker asked me if I cared to hoist a brew with him at the Mannix bar and I said why not, since no one else was being friendly.

As we walked down the Strip, the old cars tearing past us just like they were new and the sign *Call Northside 777* at what is the end of the road for us, Whittaker gave me his views on things: "It's all part of the same thing. The Watergate. The FBI. Us being caught here."

"I don't see how what's happened to us has anything to do with anything." But this wasn't true because I knew Claypoole was sent by the President. Yet if he was, why did he bad-mouth our commander-in-chief? I guess he was told Mr. Nixon had come and gone and so he felt safe. There is a mystery here.

"The connections are all there, all right. Look at that whizzer white Mrs. Bowles." The fact that the lady from Plandome has three times beaten up our tough cookie has not done his not-very-good-at-best disposition much good. "She's in with the FBI scum. And *he's* in with Mr. Williams who is a fag. Sorry, Myron."

"You got the wrong end of the steer, Whittaker," I said, getting ready to bust him. We were now at the door to the Mannix bar.

"Don't take no offense. It's just that there are some times, you got to admit, when you're . . . well . . ."

In a fairly friendly way we hoisted a couple brews together, with me all the while trying to treat coolly Myra's friends and she has a good many in that low bar, including the owner old Mannix himself who leaned over me as he passed and said, "Hey, gorgeous!"

Well, I gave him a look which if you could wrap

it around your average Mafioso hood would have anchored him to the bottom of Lake Arrowhead until the cows came home. But Mannix had moved on to serve a table of tough-looking characters with their cheap whores. God, I miss Mary-Ann and the silky terriers.

"Myron," Whittaker was rumbling in my ear, his voice just on the verge of losing its natural, mild Philadelphia scrappleness for the hillbilly tone that always means he is getting ready to pick a fight that he always loses except sometimes with dizzy girls like Iris who though they could handle him with one arm behind their backs are excited by the brutal way he comes on and forget how soft and fat he is and how, as Iris said to me just before I came back to my lonely cabin tonight where I write these notes, "That buddy of yours can hardly get it up, all two inches of gristle that looks like it'd been trimmed from a roast by some crook butcher with his thumb on the scale or maybe it was the thumb he cut off by accident and that's Whittaker full length."

Iris has a bloody kind of imagination when she gets going. "Now, I think you're something pretty special, Myron, even though you are not absolutely *complete* down there but I got to confess that when you get yourself up in drag you are the best fun I've had around these parts in a long time. You undergo *a personality change,* did you know that?"

I said yes, I knew that, feeling pretty low. Anyway, to get back to earlier, to before Whittaker went to sleep with his head in the jukebox, he said, "The only way we-all's gonna git outta hee-yuh— You lisn'in, boy? You mindin' what Uh say?"

"Yes, Whittaker."

"—is to break in on that fruit Mistuh Williams an' hole a knie-yuf to his throw-yut till he shows us thuh way to git home."

If I am game and not a coward, Whittaker plans to pull this caper tomorrow, at sundown. We will break into Mr. Williams' hotel suite with two kitchen knives which Whittaker will get from the Mannix Motel Café kitchen where he is currently working half-time deep-frying things.

I said I'd sleep on it, and not wanting any trouble with Whittaker, I sounded like I was interested and of course maybe I am, for things are a lot more desperate for me than they are for anyone else around here. I mean how many oysters can a man eat?

19

You don't know the half of it, buster!

But good news first. Yesterday one J. D. Claypoole formerly of the FBI hit the Strip—saved by *Siren of Babylon* from what I am certain would have been an indictment for his part in the Watergate scandal so wittily foretold by Preston Sturges' *The Great McGinty* (1940). According to Claypoole (who read the good news in the *Star*) Lon Chaney, Jr., at the age of sixty-eight, has made an excellent recovery from beriberi, an illness he contracted some years ago, thus explaining the absence from the silver screen of one of its finest, most deeply American presences: the monster as square. I am almost tempted to ring up Mr. Chaney right now and congratulate him! Except that his number is sure to be unlisted and of course he has not yet caught beriberi.

And then of course we must not interfere! Ha ha! Mr. Williams will not recognize 1948 by the time I get through with it. As I change for the better this holy year, future time will be affected. Or, if I may resort to witty metaphor, as one domino is picked up and set erect, so will the next and the next be restored to an upright position.

I intend to make 1948 the hinge of history. I shall split human history in two parts to be known henceforth as *pre-Myra* and *post-Myra*. Do I need to repeat that in the post-Myra world sordid scandals like Watergate will not take place because Richard Nixon's presidency will not take place?

My fellow Americans both before and after, saved and unsaved, cut and uncut: central to my vision is the street in Carverville on the Metro lot where Andy Hardy once lived and will live again. If I succeed in this great enterprise, I vow to you that the moral rot at the center of the United States will be nipped in the bud by a society which (post-Myra) will be informed throughout by the wisdom of good Judge Hardy as played by Lewis Stone.

At the moment Lewis Stone has only five more years (pre-Myra) before translation to the big studio in the sky; yet during the half decade that currently (1948) remains to Lewis Stone he could make at least five more Hardy films and, who knows, revived in his career he might not want to cool it, aged seventy-four in 1953 (pre-Myra). But if Lewis Stone does die according to the old pre-Myra schedule, then I have a replacement ready. Hang on to your hats: Mickey Rooney will become the new Judge Hardy!

Mickey will be thirty-one in 1953 and with a bit of the old Perc Westmore in the Gray-Hair-and-Crowsfeet Department, Mickey can succeed to his father's judgeship, thus sparing future (pre-Myra) generations Mickey's truly excruciating imitations of Japanese waiters on television, a minor art form that will be dedicated (post-Myra) to the glorification of Hollywood's product while continuing to make its small yet exquisite contribution to the (pre-Myra) culture, the creation of even longer and more inventive commercials.

Meanwhile, I have begun my work. Oh, how I have begun! This is Saturday, or was. I sit in a filmly pink chiffon negligee, writing it all down in my book. Need I say I am not alone? But I shall come to that in due course.

I found out about Lon Chaney, Jr., from J. D. Claypoole, who stopped in at the Mannix bar for a drink just before noon. I was dressed in an amusing slit-skirt affair with tiger-lily design. "Wow," said J. D. "You're some looker! You live around here?"

"I'm an out-of-towner, too." I gave him my siren voice and we kicked the old ball around for a while, and it was then that I learned—after a good deal of probing—about Lon Chaney, Jr.'s recovery. "Noticed it in the papers just before I landed here."

"Lucky you."

"They got nothing on me, baby."

I simply gave him a slow slightly crooked smile like Joan Fontaine six reels into *Rebecca* and *all the way* into all-time movie greatness, unlike her sister Olivia de Havilland, whose career has been one of sad decline since *Anthony Adverse* (1936). With dedication and luck Olivia might have been a second Beulah Bondi; as it is, she must forever be known as Joan's lackluster kid sister.

When J. D. tried to pick me up in a crude way, I said, "I never thought I'd be propositioned by a G-man! I guess that makes you a real maverick, doesn't it? Sort of odd-man-in, if you get what I mean."

"And what is that that you're implying?"

"I'm implying that I thought all G-men who were loyal to J. Edgar were fruits, too."

J. D. turned blue about the mouth. "That is a Commie lie!"

"Well, it's all academic now, J. D." I got up from the bar stool, my sturdy hangbag ready for action. *"De mortuis,* as we Latin bombshells say. Anyway, let's hope J. Edgar's having a ball or two up there in the biggest closet of them all, making it with Dillinger, a plaster cast of whose rehnquist I am told your leader used to keep under his pillow."

J. D. lunged at me. I stepped lightly away. He fell with a crash off the bar stool. "See you in the movies," I trilled, with an Ann Rutherford wrinkling of my nose; and so headed for the back lot.

Did I wonder whether or not Red would show up tonight? Was I fearful that he would not? Of course I was anxious, edgy, not myself. Although I am the creatrix of this world I am also, at heart, a mere woman. One who wishes to love and be loved. To hold out my hand to a masterful man, to let him draw me close to his powerful chest, to feel strong arms about my beautiful if not entirely re-equipped-for-action body, to look up into his strong face and say, "I love you!" And then burger his blackmun off. Yes, I, too, am vulnerable, tender, insecure.

Just past the gate there is a train station where died Anna Karenina, played by one Greta Garbo, whose allure was *not* truly Hollywood as a comparison with, say, her contemporary Lana Turner would quickly demonstrate and to Miss G's disadvantage.

I crossed the tracks; stepped around the real locomotive as an equally real trolley packed with tourists comes into view. "Watch it, miss," said the driver. Obviously we locals are still visible to the out-of-towners as far into the lot as the railroad station.

Just back of the station there is a pleasant bosky dell with tall trees and thick bushes and birds twittering—and on the greensward I stumbled upon these two guys making it. Their shirts were off; their blue jeans were down to their ankles and they were lying one on top of the other rubbing back and forth like a pair of nine-year-olds.

"Well, this is a pretty how-de-do!" I thundered, handbag at the ready.

"Get lost," said the dark-haired one on the top. But the fair-haired one on the bottom knew the voice of authority when he heard it and pushed the other one off him and then they quickly pulled up their pants, allowing me a pleasant glimpse of turgid, nay, tumescent, nay, *nothing* powells: a pair of standard American rosebuds, but then, to be fair to the American rosebud, like a Christmas present, it is not the actual gift but the thought *behind* the erection that counts.

"We were just taking it easy," said the dark one, giving me a look of hate.

"You won't tell nobody, will you, lady?" The blond was nervous. "I mean we're really straight."

"Save that for the Blue Parrot." This was a shot in the

dark but it connected. Myron—the original Myron—used to know a group of slightly older queens in Manhattan who all swore that right after the war the bars of New York were filled with beauty, particularly along "the bird circuit" as it was then known; and of these legendary aviaries, the Blue Parrot on the East Side was always the most brilliantly stocked with our feathered friends.

"Are you from New York too, lady?" The blond one wanted to be friendly, fearing an indictment for an act against nature as nature is defined in the unnatural state in California.

The two young men are from New York. The dark one, Mel, is going to Columbia where he plays football, he says, and the other is his buddy Gene, a carhop, and they are traveling about the country while school is out. "We dig the road, lady," said Gene, the con man of the pair.

"You dig each other."

"Hell," said Mel, "I'm just a kind of *come on'er,* that's all."

"Come on *him* is closer to the mark, buddy."

I don't know why I thought at first that they were out-of-towners but they proved to be locals. It was exciting, I confess: two genuine sweaty 1948 youths, smelling of sex, as they talked of bop music, of hipsters, of smoking tea . . . tea! That dear old pre-mainline word! They were, they said, *beat.* Yes, that word was born in the bosky dell of Metro's back lot or at least revealed for the first time to me as though for my blessing, which I gave.

Mel said, "I guess you might say that I am—that we're both—sort of beat with life, with everything."

"Not Hollywood surely."

"L.A. is keating," said Gene. "We been holed up on South Main where the police bust you every two minutes and the women is all whores."

"Not all of us." I was, I fear, revoltingly saccharine but something about those two studs touched me. After all, I was witnessing the dawn of Beat.

Mel was conciliating. "You're a right beautiful woman,

ma'am," he said respectfully. "But what we're after is this pure thing that's beyond sex. You dig Céline?"

"I do *not* read novels." I was suddenly hard. "The only words that I care for are dialogue. Get it? High-priced Metro dialogue is all I need words-wise, so you can take your Céline and shove his collected works all the way up that long journey to the end of the night in your blackmun."

Well, that had the effect of inspiring terror and awe. They both started trembling and, though swathed in denim, their rosebuds were plainly contracting to acorn proportions. As is my policy, after the whammy, the softening up. "I confess that in my day I have studied the enemy, contemplated the strategies of fiction if only in order to find new ways to destroy the art form whose only distinction is that it prepared the way for the movies, much as John the B. prepared the way for big J. C. And of course I will never deny the importance of *any* novel which has been used to inspire a work of celluloid. We are all permanently indebted to James Hilton, Daphne du Maurier and W. Somerset Maugham, whose names head the golden list. Yet at best their works are no more than so much grit beneath the studio's shell: mere occasions for masterpieces, for cinema pearls."

I could see that I had completely overwhelmed them; and was pleased. Unfortunately (for him), Mel still had a little starch left in him. "But I don't think that's true, ma'am. I mean words, wowee, that's all we got, my buddies and me with these long talks we have about perception and really *seeing* just what it is this cosmos-thing sees and all the beatness of it, the beatitude, yeah, that's the word for all the words we say, for all this yakking we do."

"Stop!" I commanded. I had had a sudden vision—like Jennifer when she saw Linda in *The Song of Bernadette*— of the post-Myra world which I now realize that I must devise a *precise* blueprint for. To date, I confess, I have been creating the future in an inexcusably haphazard fashion, but in my defense I must note the extenuating circumstance that I lack not only a well-trained staff but mobility. "Mel, you must write all this keating down."

"Keating?" whined Mel, but Gene stopped him, muttering, 'Don't get the lady mad. Watch out for that handbag. There's lead in it."

"Like in your pistol, Gene?" I was jocose. Buddy buddy. I needed them. "Yes, write it down. Make a book of it. Call it a novel, if you like."

"But I thought you said I was to take all the novels and shove them . . ."

"Please, Mel. That is an offensive image to use in the presence of a lady. I mean that I can predict absolute success for your work at this time. *But* you must beat—that word again!—Kerouac to the punch."

"Who?"

"If you do as I say, Mel, your name will be up there on the screen, and *his* will be unknown. Can't you see it, Mel? *Based on a novel by Mel American Rosebud . . .*"

"But that's not my name."

"Because—this year—I promise that Metro, *my* studio" —I indicated the Thalberg Building, which I cannot see but they could—"will begin a series of films about hipsters, hot-rodders, lovers of boogie-woogie, not to mention belly-rubbing . . ."

"Belly-rubbing?" This blew Gene's mind.

"What do you think you two pro-crypto fags were doing just now?"

"But we dig the broads," squeaked Gene, jumping to avoid the handbag with which I had intended to reduce to an ounce of attar his tiny rosebud.

"Of course you do! You're part of my vision for this studio. And—now get this—if we can have your story on the screen by 1950, as a vehicle for Van Johnson and Peter Lawford, camera work by James Wong Howe and directed by any one of our staff directors, though I might bring in Irving Rapper from Warner's, I will be able to start a cycle of profitable pix that will knock the quiz shows out of the box and off the tube and fill the movie houses of the world with a new sort of film, more wondrous than anything as yet dreamed of even by Herbert Yates. A *beat* generation is what I will give the movie audience first. But a beat generation that is well groomed, exquisitely lit, and acted by major stars in perfect frames. Here is my card." I had—as always—written my name on the back of a cocktail napkin and stuffed it in my purse just in case.

I gave it to the stunned Mel.

"Now mop the come off your jeans, boys. Mel, you dictate into the nearest recorder that tome which, I promise you, Irving Lazar will see is bought to my studio for a sum in the high six figures. Gene, you will be inked, too, as tech. adviser."

They fled me, grateful for the vision I had given them of a new world. We shall hear from Mel, I am sure of that.

So, Mr. Williams, I have begun to alter this year of grace, *my* grace, and if I can film a photoplay with a title that has Beat in it—*On Beat, Beat Me Daddy Eight to the Bar, The Beat Years of Our Lives, The Beat Man, Beat Your Meat*—I will anticipate and torpedo an entire "literary" movement of the pre-Myra fifties when the so-called Beat writers, howling their words at random, helped distract attention from our Industry's product and made it possible for Charles Van Doren to dominate through television the entire culture, answering questions whose answers he had been given in advance—a twenty-one-inch corruption that was directly responsible, first, for the death of Marilyn Monroe at the hands of the two Kennedys and, second, for R. M. Nixon's current subversion of the government. Fortunately I—and I alone—can turn America around. It is a great responsibility and one to which I intend to rise, humbly of course but inexorably.

Meanwhile, right in front of me, there is something else for me to turn around. I shall, in a few minutes, create the first fun-loving sterile Amazon. Ether, scalpel, Lysol, sutures, Mercurochrome, clamps, silicone, needle and thread are ready. So is Red, who arrived at nine-oh-five in the bar of the Mannix Motel.

I am half in love with Red—or should I call him Steve Dude, his acting name? Stark naked, Steve is on his tum-tum, hands and feet handcuffed to the metal headboard and footboard; a pillow beneath his tum-tum not only makes for added viewing pleasure but, according to the medical dictionary, it is the classic position for the removal of unwanted powells. I have not of course told him what I have in mind for him. I am in a mischievous trick-or-treat mood.

Steve is looking at me, as I write, and I detect in his round blue eyes not only true passion but tenderness of the sort I have needed all my life. Once he is not Steve but Stefanie—my best girl friend—we will be inseparable pals, like Constance and Norma Talmadge.

The gag which I made for him using an old bra and one of his socks has slipped down to his chin, revealing the full sensual lips of a second Maureen O'Hara . . .

20

Jesus Christ, Myra is going to get me killed or put in jail on a sodomy rap for life and *she* would damn well deserve it though I am innocent, I swear.

Suddenly just now I find myself sitting at this table in this motel cabin dressed in a slinky dressing gown with a padded bra underneath and holding a pencil in my *left* hand which maybe explains why I can't read what she writes in this notebook because I am right-handed while handcuffed to the bed is this naked red-haired kid.

I just sat and stared at him and he stared at me, obviously scared out of his wits as who would not be if he's fallen into Myra's clutches? It took me, oh, maybe five minutes to get it together in my own head.

As per usual I tried to see into Myra's mind and as per usual I got nowhere at all. Whatever she does or thinks is just a blackout for me. Each time I come back I pick up where I left off last time—not to mention having to pick up the pieces *she's* left lying around and let me tell you, Steve Dude is about the biggest piece of all so far and I am still stunned even shook up by the enormity of Myra's crime against this boy's nature not to mention my own.

"What's your name?" I asked in my normal voice.

"Steve Dude like I told you, Myra." The voice cracked as if Steve was your average teenager though he is at least twenty-one—that is, I pray to God he is twenty-one and not a minor with all the problems I would then have to face like twenty years in Alcatraz.

"I'm sorry about this, Steve."

"Oh, that's O.K. I really didn't mind. Sincerely, Myra."

He was lying and willing to say anthing to get the hell out of there. How Myra had managed to overpower this six foot two one hundred eighty pound stud is something I do not want to think about. Any more than I want to know what she was going to do with him. The sharp knife I found in the top bureau drawer I took and buried behind the cabin and the Lysol and the ether I poured in the sink. I couldn't open the bottom bureau drawer which is locked. Anyway, I am certain she couldn't've wanted to do what I think she wanted to do.

"Where did she . . ." But then I decided it would be too complicated to explain to Steve my situation. He seems sort of dumb, with a Texas accent like Whittaker likes to put on only Steve's is for real since he is from Beaumont.

"I seem to've forgotten where I put the keys." I pointed to the handcuffs. He looked up at me as if he thought I was about to turn into Charles Manson or something.

"I reckon they're still in the pocket of your robe, Myra, where you put them."

So they were. I took a deep breath and crossed to the bed, keys in hand. What I was about to do was pretty risky. Though no man is a match for Myra, who does know a bit of judo and has the strength of ten, I am just your ordinary guy with the strength of one who is getting kind of out of shape in the Valley

GORE VIDAL

particularly since the Vic Tanney Studio down the road shut down a few years back. Steve could do me a lot of damage if he was in a bad mood.

Well, I decided that I would just have to take that chance and rely on his memory of whatever it was that Myra did in the first place to get him in the fix he was in and be too scared to do anything violent.

I undid the handcuffs first from his ankles (how did Myra manage to get ahold of handcuffs in the first place?). Modestly he put his legs together even though he didn't need to because no power on earth could have got me to look at his spread cheeks. I did not want to know anything, *repeat* anything, about what that monster did.

"I'm sorry about this," I said and I really meant it as I unlocked the handcuff first from his left then from his right wrist. "I really am. It's just that I get sort of carried away sometimes."

"Oh, that's O.K." The relief on his face was like the sun coming up over the prairie. I stood back from the bed, automatically crouching down just in case he threw a punch in my direction, but Myra had really done her work whatever it was.

Steve just lay there a minute or two on the bed, rubbing his wrists. Then he rolled over and sat up on the edge of the bed, modestly crossing his legs and putting his hands in his lap but not before I had a look at his very large equipment (thank God, undamaged) and also took in the fact that all his pubic hair had been shaved away.

Steve blushed when he saw where I was staring and said, "You really give a clean shave, Myra."

Why had Myra shaved him? And why . . .? No, I don't want to know. "So it seems," I said, pretty embarrassed too.

"Well," said Steve. "I guess I better be on my way."

"I guess so," I said, suddenly wanting just to lie

down and go to sleep until I get out of this nightmare and am home again.

"Can I put my clothes on now?"

"Oh, yes, Steve. Yes. Please." I was flustered and probably more upset than he was if that was possible.

Quickly Steve pulled on an old army shirt, wrinkled chinos, white sweat socks, one of which had been used to gag him with, and desert boots.

"Well," he said, ready to leave, "I guess there's a first time for everything."

Of course I didn't know what he meant though of course I really did know or could've made like they say at important press conferences an educated guess. "So it was really your first time?" I heard myself say from far off. I am developing a sort of echo chamber in my head.

"Jesus, couldn't you tell? Anyway, I'm sorry about yelling the way I did. I mean that sincerely."

My heart skipped—is skipping beats. My hands are still clammy. "I guess she—I guess I wasn't very gentle."

"Could I see that thing you used? The dill—what do you call that thing?"

"Dildo." I croaked the word and knew then just what it was Myra had done. She had pretended to sodomize Steve with a dildo when, in fact, she had actually used Dr. Mengers' powerful rehnquist which is almost too large for your average experienced female or male much less for a boy who is a virgin in that department which Steve is, or was, poor bastard.

I stammered something about how what with the damp night air and all I had locked the dildo up for the night, all the while wondering why Steve didn't turn violent and beat the dickens out of me. Myra sure has it coming to her. But I guess Steve was still scared to death of Myra and, craziest of all, he's still very much intrigued by her from what he had to say before he left. "I just hope you won't have to do that again. I mean I'm really, like you say, broken in now, and I mean that sincerely."

"Oh, never, never again!" This was from the heart.

"Because to tell the truth I didn't really feature it too much."

"I understand. I really do!"

"I mean I've cornholed a few li'l ole gals in my time and I always believed 'em when they *said* it was O.K. and didn't hurt too much though I'm a fair-sized man, you know."

"I know you are, Steve."

" 'Course I never in my wildest dreams dreamed any li'l ole gal would ever come along and cornhole *me*."

"Well, live and learn." I was just gabbling anything that came into my head.

"But I tell you one thing. If any guy ever did that to me, why, I'd track him down to the end of the earth and I'd kill him. I sincerely would and that's a promise." Steve looked mighty mean when he said this which is about as mean as they come since in his clothes he looks like quite a lot of potentially tough guy, very different from the scared boy I first saw on the bed with his wounded blackmun wide open to every breeze that blows.

"Well, Steve, we girls"—how I hated having to put on that act but I am not about to get killed for Myra's crimes—"like our little games."

"I'll say. You know it was kinda like an enema with a blowtorch."

"But it wasn't so awfully bad, was it? I mean you did like *some* of it, didn't you, Steve."

"Myra, I hated every last minute of what you did, and that's the absolute truth so help me God, sincerely."

"Sorry" was the best I could do, as I sort of edged him out of the cabin.

"I still don't know why you shaved me like that."

"To . . . uh, to control your prickly heat, dear."

"Well, I'll be waitin' for your next message, Myra. Will it be . . . uh, sent like the other one was?"

What other message? What was he talking about? "Yes, yes," I said, anything to get him out of the cabin.

"Jesus H. Christ!" Steve said and shaking his head he jumped into his Plymouth convertible which was parked beside the "Vacancy" sign and drove off into the night while I came back in here and sat down to write in this book only to notice that pressed between the leaves of an earlier section were quantities of Steve's red hair from his crotch which I just now got rid of.

When I came back from the bathroom who should be sitting on the bed but Whittaker, half plastered and looking for trouble which I was not in the mood to give him having been, let me say, shocked and shook up by the whole Steve Dude business.

"Look at you!" Whittaker pointed at my wig, makeup, dressing gown.

I'm afraid I was every bit as disgusted as he was but I was not about to pick a fight. "Get lost," I said quietly.

"And what were you doing to that man in there? Why was he screaming?"

"So you're a wiretapper as well as a ptomaine peddler."

"You don't need no electronic bug to hear what I heard."

"Why don't you get your blackmun out of here, Whittaker?"

"You forgot what night this is?"

I could no more have told him what night it was than I could get into the movie house down the road and see *Call Northside 777*. For all I knew, Myra might've been at the controls for weeks.

Well, I learned that she hasn't been around all that long and that tonight is the night when Whittaker and I were suppose to break in on Mr. Williams and force him to get us out of here. "He's got this place under his thumb. He knows every entrance *and* every exit."

I didn't tell Whittaker that I know more or less where one of the exits is but I don't think I'm going to be able to find it on my own and I don't expect Luke or the Negro will be very helpful. Anyway, I don't want to tangle with them, particularly Luke.

Whittaker kept rambling on. "If we stay here much longer it's cancer."

"Cancer?"

"Yes, you dumb queen! Can't you tell? This place is giving us all cancer. This is where it all started. I got it pinpointed to right after the war when all the cancer-causing agents go loose in spite of Saran wrap. Those food additives. And television. The hormones in the chicken and beef. Myron, we're in cancer gulch."

Whittaker went on making this crazy connection between cancer and food and what he calls his existential vision of the last big connection which is between lard, I think he said, and sex but by then he had lost me and I kicked him out with a promise to reconsider the plan to kidnap or threaten to kidnap Mr. Williams in order to get out of here because if I don't get out of here soon and back under the care of a good physician I will not only lose all control to Myra who will never leave this place if I know her, not to mention probably getting killed by one of these 1948 local boys who are tough war veterans and not like the soft youth of America today who, due to the coddling they got as babies from Dr. Spock and other Communist sympathizers, were unable to stem the rise of Communism in Southeast Asia and so let down our President in his quest for peace with honor, forcing him to abandon the democratic and *freely* elected government in Saigon to the mercies of Hanoi, and to the yellow hordes of Central Asia, thus explaining the fact that he looked very unwell the other day when he was here, particularly when he took off his Nixon mask.

Next day.

Dressed in my denim cowboy-style duds and nervous because I know that I am now thanks to Myra your average pariah on the Strip, I went into the lobby of the Thalberg Hotel where Mrs. Connally Yarborough Bowles was playing canasta with three out-of-town ladies from the mid-fifties when that game was all the rage.

I'm afraid the ladies pretended not to see me as I went on over to the desk where Chicken was in charge. He looked kind of pale when he saw me, the usual effect Myra has on young males, and even though I am Myron and straight as a die I guess it shows through, her terrible lust, her desire to take over everybody, everything in the world, and in this case I was truly sorry because I could imagine a real sort of palship between Chicken Van Upp and yours truly, consisting of us two fishing for trout in one of your nearby streams, skinny-dipping together in the old swimming hole the way it used to be when a man and a boy and a dog, too, sometimes, could have real relationship without your real boy like Chicken ending up stuffed from behind like an olive with a pimento like Steve Dude.

"I'd like to talk to Rooster, Chicken," I said.

"Pa!" yelled Chicken; and skedaddled.

Rooster entered the lobby from the office, smiling and frowning at the same time like always. "Mr. Breckinridge—I presume?"

"Yes, you presume right. I want to see Mr. Williams."

"Write your name in this book . . ."

"I've written my name in that book ten times. Now I want to see him or there will be real trouble around here." I noticed something odd then. There is a mirror behind where Rooster was standing and in the mirror

I could see the canasta players. Well, Rooster looked over my shoulder at Mrs. C. Y. Bowles and she gave him a nod and a high sign—that is, made a circle with thumb and forefinger.

"O.K., Mr. Breckinridge. I'll do my best. Come this way."

I followed Rooster up to the first floor and down the corridor to a door with a metal plaque in it which said *Mr. Williams.* "That's a pretty old plaque," I said, pointing to the tarnish on the brass and how the letters are getting a bit dim from too much polishing over the years.

"Mr. Williams brought it with him." Rooster was smooth. "And we put it up in June when he got here. We think the world of Mr. Williams around here." Rooster peered at the plaque. "Needs a bit of elbow grease. You're right." Then Rooster rapped on the door and Mr. Williams said, "Come!"

Rooster opened the door a crack; put his head in. "It's Mr. Breckinridge. Mayday! Mayday!"

"I read you, Rooster. Carry on."

Rooster stood back and I went into the sitting room of Mr. Williams' so-called luxurious suite and it was really pretty swell-looking with bookcases packed from floor to ceiling with thousands, I'd guess, of books and a crystal-type chandelier in the center of the ceiling and a big gold desk just under it and a big chair near the window that looks out onto Thalberg Boulevard and, yes, a telescope at the window through which Mr. Williams obviously keeps track of us out-of-towners.

The door shut behind and the key was turned in the lock.

I was alone with Mr. Williams, who turned out to be the Negro who had been so snotty to our President. Mr. Williams is as black as the ace of spades and looks just like old photos of Father Refined I think he was called, who was short and stocky and bald with a gold-toothed smile and used to give away fried chicken at his Heaven in Harlem during the Depression, serving even honkies like my mother Gertrude the practical nurse who went there when she was broke.

"Do come in, please. Sit down." Mr. Williams was graciousness itself and I responded in kind although I cannot say I have been too happy about the prospect of a black mayor of Los Angeles, a current (1973) possibility. What with property values already seriously endangered by taxes together with having the coloreds start to move into the various neighborhoods would further depress the sole capital investment of many middle-income *completely* tolerant people like me who happen to be white and who oppose busing just on practical and not, I repeat *not,* on racist grounds.

I sat down in the chair opposite the big leather chair where Mr. Williams had been reading *The Federalist Papers*, something from school I recall. Within easy reach was the telescope. He smiled when he saw what I was looking at. "Yes, I must keep an eye out for new arrivals. Our people don't always catch them, you know, at the usual entrances. Might I offer you a cordial?" If you shut your eyes you'd think from listening to Mr. Williams that he was white.

After he had poured us two small shots of something pretty awful, I said, "Well, I guess you probably know why I'm here . . ."

"Concerned all of us who are good Americans." Mr. Williams was talking right through me as if he hadn't heard me. "It is my view, Mr. Breckinridge, based on the latest reports, particularly the valuable presentation of J. D. Claypoole Friday night, that the President will be forced by events and by world opinion to resign."

This was about the last subject I had on my mind which is filled with nothing but homesickness for Mary-Ann and the dogs and fear of Myra and Steve Dude though if I could go fishin' with Chicken—no, cancel that last. It is now inoperative as it could be misinterpreted because something basically fine and noble would look suspicious to anyone who associated Myron who is a straight shooter with that monster as who couldn't help doing on the Strip?

Nevertheless I rose to the defense of *our* President. "Mr. Nixon has not been in any way directly connected with the break-in at the Watergate or with the later attempted cover-up by certain of his highly motivated associates who in their love for America and our institutions perhaps went too far in ensuring the re-election of what, after all, has proved to be a winning combination Dick, Pat, Tricia, Julie, David, Cox . . ."

Well, I had a lot more to say to Mr. Williams who even though he *sounds* like he's white when you shut your eyes is black as the ace of spades when you open them and so is naturally opposed to our President who had put his people—Mr. Williams' people—on notice that until they stop their crime in the streets and having children on welfare and start to make for themselves the kind of strong family structure which is essential in a true democracy they will continue to enjoy the benign neglect they deserve. I happen to have read up at length on this problem in the *Los Angeles Times* as well as in *Reader's Digest*.

"I fear we must agree to disagree," said Mr. Williams. "Now your problem, I gather—"

"In one word is O-U-T. I want out, Mr. Williams."

"So do we all."

"No. You've been here twenty-three years—I saw that name plate outside, it's about worn thin—and you've got a good thing going just like all the others, living the same eight weeks in the summer of '48 over and over and over again, no wonder you're all nuts."

"'Nuts'?" Mr. Williams looked real polite and snotty at the same time. "Mr. Breckinridge, if you will forgive me, I don't believe that the behavior of any member of our little band can compare for sheer *eccentricity* to your own."

Well, that was score one for your high-toned nigger

and I didn't have much of a comeback, not knowing how much he knows about Myra's activites—not knowing myself. "I have these moods," I said, trying to sound as offhand as possible. "Comedy routines I have worked out in many clubs around the Valley."

"Your comedy of last night was unusually well received by the young man you were entertaining in your cabin. His, uh, 'laughter' could be heard from one end of the Strip to the other."

"Well, he was a quick study like they say. I was just teaching him a few routines, and it was breaking him up."

"Let me repeat, Mr. Breckinridge. Rule one: You must not try to alter anything here. If you do, you derange or damage the future, and perhaps destroy us all."

"Mr. Williams, I will alter everything, including blowing up the back lot and keeping the world from ever seeing *Siren of Babylon* to get out of this place and home again."

"Oh, dear." Mr. Williams was suspiciously mild. He acts as if my threats mean nothing. *As if there is nothing that I can do to alter anything* which is a pretty horrible thought. Has he met me before like this? "Perhaps you need a—well, a hobby, a distraction, other than the amusing *impressions en travestie* that you delight us with from time to time."

"Such as?"

"Literature, Mr. Breckinridge." A black fist indicated the shelves of Heritage Club masterpieces in rich gilt-edged genuine plastileather. "I am devoting my time here—the remaining two weeks I have in this quiet part of the world—to reading all of the world's great literature. All of it that I can read in two weeks of course. Yes." He laughed as if he had said or was going to say something funny. "For me, even as we speak, the golden bowel has begun ever so slightly to most beautifully crack." Whatever that meant. It sounds like that complaint of Gertrude's in recent years which is spelled "diverticulitis."

"I've got nothing against reading books when there's time which is not much considering my busy schedule and how tired I am at night when we turn on the TV, Mary-Ann and I."

"Alas, we have no proper TV here. Even the sinister Milton Berle has not yet begun his mission. But there are films to contemplate."

"I hate movies. I'm not . . ." I was going to say "Myra" but I stopped myself. "Anyway, we can't even get in to see *Call Northside 777* down the road while *The Three Musketeers* won't open, even if we could get in, until after . . . after we're gone from here. Isn't that right?"

"Yes." I did not like all this stillness that Mr. Williams let surround the one word.

"Except we're *not* going away from here because we start the picture all over again."

"Yes." More stillness; black as ink, his face.

"Mr. Williams, you've been through the shooting of this film twenty-three times. Once for each year since you checked in."

"Yes."

"Each year you go from the last day of shooting July 31, 1948, to the first day of shooting June 1, 1948."

"Yes."

"You started doing all this in 1950."

"Yes."

"So for twenty-three years you've been going from June 1 to July 31, and back again."

"Yes."

"Well, explain me this little thing. Time is passing outside. There are new arrivals most every day which is how you've been able to keep up with what's happening back there like your very radical remarks about our President to me just now suggested. Well, if this is the same eight-week period which it has to be for everybody who's really in 1948, then how can it change with each passing year for us since nearly every day someone is arriving from the future and on the day he arrives somebody else has probably arrived that same day, too, but the year before or the year before that and so on back to 1950?" I am going mad, I think, as I try to think things through and write them down in this account book.

"Well, are we all coming here at once?" I asked. "And if everybody is, then the last arrival, but I mean the very *last* person ever to catch *Siren of Babylon* on the Late Late Show and get caught in it, is already here, and the game is up. But who is it? Who is the last one, and what happens to everybody when he gets here?"

"Is the universe infinite or finite? If it is infinite, there is no last."

"This is a con game, Mr. Williams, and you are the number one-con around here."

"Mr. Breckinridge, I promise that in time, yes, within our eight-week *pousse-café* of days, you will adapt as we all have, as we all must." But as he said this I saw that same strange look in his eye that I had noticed in Rooster's eye when he looked past me at Mrs. C. Y. Bowles with a questioning look but also with a troubled look and with—well, with this *frightened* look. I think they think if I start rocking the boat I might in some way wreck their little game whatever it is. I hope they are right but I don't know how in hell to really start rocking. The possibility I am the last person to arrive here went through my head, but how could I be when J. D. Claypoole has more news of the Watergate than anybody?

"Feel free," said Mr. Williams, "to call on me at any time. Just check with Rooster . . ."

"Who must be pushing seventy now that it's 1973."

'But it's only 1948, as you can plainly see. And that, I fear, is all that it will ever be for us. Or for

Rooster—this summer anyway. Good day, Mr. Breckinridge."

I had a lot more to say but I saw it was no good. As I started toward the door, the phone rang and Mr. Williams answered it. "Hello, L. B.," he said. "Yes, I've read the script. *The Miniver Story* has everything!"

I shut the door behind me wondering if the L.B. he was talking to was really L. B. Mayer and if so is Mr. Williams in the pay of the studio, to help them read books maybe. It is very clear to me that he is not your average nigger by a long shot.

I went out to the Thalberg pool where I found Iris in her one-piece Jantzen with the small tit built up to match the big one which I suppose is easier to do than to squeeze the big one down to the size of the small one.

She was chatting with Mr. Telemachus who was fully clothed, drinking a beer and holding a copy of weekly *Variety,* the bible of show business.

"Word's got around," he said, not in a very nice way I thought. "You've been up to see Mr. Williams."

"What's he like?" Iris was sitting cross-legged beside the pool, careful to hold in her stomach. She is a good-looking girl and though I never thought I'd cheat on Mary-Ann, I feel that these are highly extenuating circumstances and I need Iris to keep me a hundred-percent normal guy in a hundred-percent abnormal situation.

"Black," I said, meaning to be nasty too.

"So I've heard," said Mr. Telemachus.

"I saw him once a few years back," said Iris, "at least I *thought* it was him and he looked more, you know, South American or Mexican."

"How could you have seen him several years ago when he only checked in the first of June?" I was going to get to the bottom of all this or burst.

"Easy, fella," said Mr. Telemachus, doing John Carradine.

"There you two go!" Iris was ecstatic. "Talking that funny talk of yours."

"What did what I just said sound like?"

"Careful!" From Mr. Telemachus.

"Don't ask *me* when *you* know! I mean you're the one talking crazy talk."

Well, we were getting nowhere and what with one thing and another and my being nervous I went up to Iris's room and had, all in all, a good time though I was kind of shocked even shook up when just before we got started she said, "Why, look at your poor rehnquist! How red and raw it is! What've you been doing, you bad boy?"

"I could never explain in a million years," I said, wanting to murder, yes, murder Myra who without so much as a by-your-leave went and used Dr. Mengers' remarkable rehnquist to burger Steve Dude's obviously very tight and plainly Brillo-y blackmun and then left *me* to have to live not only with a raw and fairly sensitive rehnquist (at least on the underside where the skin from my wrist is) but with the possibility that Steve himself might come back at any time to get even.

Somewhat relaxed by my meeting with Iris, I went on the back lot to look for the exit. Just past the Andy Hardy street, I ran into Maude who was escorting this dazed-looking new arrival, a woman of perhaps thirty in a negligee and holding a glass half full of whiskey, the way she had been holding it while watching the Late Late Show.

I should say here that I am one of the few people ever to arrive fully clothed since most people who are caught by *Siren of Babylon* are either in their pajamas or underwear or stark naked as it is late at night or early in the A.M. for them when they hit the Strip. There is a special wardrobe and makeup room in one of the Chinese pagodas left over from *The Good Earth* where the naked ones are given bathrobes and slippers so that they can cross the boulevard without getting arrested.

Maude was delighted with the newcomer, Helen Bird of Jackson, Michigan. "Helen is a beautician with the latest news of *Vogue* and she tells me Mr. Kenneth is absolutely nowhere as of today—May 16, 1973," said Maude, remembering his manners and introducing Helen Bird.

"April 17, 1973," I answered—and realize as I write this down while waiting for the scene where the exit is to come up that it has been one month now that I have been separated from Mary-Ann though only about two weeks here.

"Oh, God. God!" Helen Bird started to sob as she finished off her drink.

"This girl didn't spill a single drop even while going through the *CREDITS*." Maude was very admiring.

"What am I doing here?" Helen Bird was not only confused but she was drunk as altogether too many out-of-towners who watch late-night television tend to be upon arrival.

Luckily, along came Mrs. Connolly Yarborough Bowles dressed for badminton. "Thank you, Maude. For a job well done. I will take the lady in charge. To register her. To see to her special wants."

Helen Bird and Mrs. C. Y. Bowles then fell into one another's arms and had a good cry as Mrs. C. Y. Bowles led the very upset plastered lady to be registered at the Thalberg Hotel.

"Maude," I said, "what happens when you come back to the day you first arrived?"

There it was again. That tricky *knowing* look. This time from behind Maude's giant dark glasses.

"I don't understand, sweetie."

"Maude." I held Maude's fat round neck in between my pretty large strong hands. "I suggest you play ball, Maude." I was quiet but menacing. "Answer my question. What happened when *you* came back again to that first day when you arrived?"

"That's it! I *arrived*, sweetie. That's all." Maude squealed and tried to get away.

"I mean, Maude, what happened on the first anniversary of your arrival?"

"Eight weeks is hardly a year, sweetie."

"Maude, I am going to start squeezing your fat neck right here on the Strip and if you don't want a pair of ugly bruises which not even Max Factor can cover up on your neck, you better tell me what happened."

"You come through again." Maude sounded frightened, and not so much of me as of the second floor of the Thalberg Hotel where the telescope was trained on the two of us. "You're not supposed to know. Nobody's supposed to know until it happens. It's a rule. You come through like the first time."

A moment of hope. "Does that mean you go *back?* So that you can come through again?"

"No. You just go back to where you first came in. For you that's the Grand Staircase. Now, sweetie, do stop crushing my blouse."

I let my hands fall. "Then what happens?"

"Why, nothing. You just keep on."

"Just like before?" I was getting scared, let me tell you. The vibrations are getting worse around here by the minute. I could feel Mr. Williams' telescope practically burning a hole in the back of my neck.

"Well, of course like before." That was what I call evasive.

"Maude, is *every*thing repeated?" This was the question that I was too scared to ask before because I was too scared even to face the possibility that *we just go round and round doing the same thing over and over again.*

"No, silly!" Straightening his clothes, Maude backed away with a last sneaky look at the telescope. "It's always different."

"Except for coming back once every eight weeks . . ."

"Well, yes. And some other things repeat. Little things. Oh, you'd hardly notice. After all, there's always somebody *new* arriving. Like Helen Bird who has given beauty treatments to all the Ford girls when she was working at Grosse Point near the country club where—what a hoot!—they wouldn't let Christina Ford in because they didn't know it was her! Oh, Helen Bird has a fund of fun stories!"

Then Maude was gone and I went on into the movie where I am now waiting for the Grand Staircase scene to come around in another forty minutes.

Sudden light goes on in my head. How did Maude have time to hear so many stories from Helen Bird about the Fords in Grosse Pointe when the Helen Bird I just met is absolutely drunk and makes no sense?

Maude had brought Helen Bird in before. That is the plain awful truth and that means I'll have to start meeting everybody for the "first" time again as soon as I make my first re-entry. But I'll get out of here first.

21

No, you won't! Ever. Long before the Grand Staircase scene I was myself again.

The insufferable Myron has an uncanny ability to reappear when he's least wanted (as if he is ever wanted by anyone save the mongoloid Mary-Ann). I had hardly got past the prelude to the fugue that was to transform Steve Dude into Stefanie Dude when Myron re-entered the atmosphere, as we say at Cape Canaveral, and stayed my hand, thus depriving the world, temporarily, of Stefanie and 1974's world famine.

Worse, it is going to take me hours to rebuild my *maquillage*, which now includes false eyelashes exactly like those worn by Miliza Korjus in *The Great Waltz* (a favorite film by the late Marshal Stalin) as well as an Ilona Massey beauty mark on my chin. Need I say that the totel effect is now ravishing, even without my once and future silicone father hills?

I have made up my mind that if the plastic surgeon in Culver City has not come back from Lake Arrowhead in time, I shall make a date with another surgeon farther afield—in Brentwood, say, and go under the knife June 1 which will give me eight weeks in which to become whole again. I assume of course that the local beauty-butchers and blowers of silicone make house calls. If not, then I assume that I shall be able to *persuade* one of them to do what I want him to do, since it is not possible for me to fail. In this I resemble God at the moment he created the universe with a single fart. Yes, I am happy to give my imprimatur to the big-bang theory that is generally accepted as being the first movement of the music of this and all the other spheres.

But I have now begun to outdo the prime mover himself as I weave this cage of old time, salvaged from the cloacal confusions of that mindless universe the first mover has so wisely surrendered to me. Slowly, carefully I now draw to myself the very stuff and essence of all time, pulling from heaven's farthest limit those strands of aging light whose golden surfaces reflect the entire history of a billion stars which like so many fireflies have been extinguished, drowned, sucked into the last *FADE OUT* which is *FADE IN* to the other, to the negative universe beyond the quasars and the pulsars of our knowing, beyond that unbelievable weight of total darkness where, until the opening of my eyes, our race's imagination always came full stop and there was nothing until I saw fit to reshape past, present and future in my own image as there can be no other if we are to survive as the regnant species.

Right off, I must change the décor of *Siren of Babylon*. Then I shall present to various interested parties the notes I have been making all afternoon on how to save Metro from Kerkorian and Aubrey by re-establishing the studio as of this date (1948) to its rightful place as principal purveyor of the world's dreams. This means that I—and I alone—shall determine *what* is dreamed by the human race within this cage of time through whose radiant bars only I can view eternity just as I am now —at this very instant—creating the cage itself.

On the back of one of Myron's dumb Chinese fortunes I wrote "Wednesday night. Same time, place. Bring director. M."

During the long commercial and station break in the middle of the Execution of the Guilty Priestess Scene during which Steve looks his very best as one of the guards standing at attention behind Louis Calhern's throne, I got down to business. Yes, I have interfered and changed the future.

As I hurried onto the set, I was conscious of a sudden overwhelming blast of what I can only think was purest ozone—so the earth's air must have been when human life first stirred in the loins of some mute mutancy.

I crossed to Steve, who was frozen into attitude, mouth slightly—and I fear a bit stupidly—open. I pulled up his Babylonian skirt; yanked the ancient jockstrap to one side and saw with delight *proof* of my intervention, my power to restructure the universe and re-create *Siren of Babylon* as well as the human race: the pubic hairs were gone and I knew what I needed to know—that this scene was shot *after* our meeting at the Mannix Motel. From the length of the rough stubble in his rosy crotch (the prickly heat was going away), I guessed that three days had passed since our first meeting.

Briskly I slipped back the foreskin I had come to know so well (to the creatrix of new worlds *not* to indulge in such detail is to commit the only indecency, gasseous critics notwithstanding); inserted my *billet-doux*; recovered the delicate violet-colored rehn, which in a state of erection becomes a stormy dark purple like the volcano in *The Hurricane* (Jon Hall, Dorothy Lamour; 1937) and thus provides a vivid color-contrast to those feather-induced white jets that on Saturday night arched into the air as high as his chin during an early phase of that initiation for which he had been prepared from the top, regarding me, quite correctly, as someone supernatural because—this was said while we were still in the bar and his ordeal not yet begun, "Golly, I just don't know how you was able to get that Chinese fortune to—well, to where you did." I witnessed the first of many blushes. "I mean, Jesus H. Christ, you must've given me a knockout drop or something on the set or in the dressing room during makeup to be able to put that thing where you did."

I gave him a mysterious smile. "Myra has her little ways, not to mention her plans, her *big* plans for you, Steve Dude, star-to-be."

Chuckling to myself as I recalled the scene, I took from my handbag a bit of pink ribbon and tied it in a bow around the tip of his rather longer than average foreskin. Then I let his skirt fall back in place.

I looked at my watch: three minutes to go before the station break ended. Time enough to alter time.

I went over to the priestess who is about to be executed and unsnapped her gilded breastplate to reveal a pair of father hills as fine as any ever fondled by L. B. Mayer during the lunch hour at—or under—his desk in the Thalberg Building.

I then undid the girl's hair in such a way that each nipple was hidden by the horsehair wig someone in makeup had created for her, obviously working on the cheap in order to keep for himself the human hair assigned for the job. Presently I shall put a stop to this petty pilferage.

I was nearly caught in the scene. But the tugging sensation began just in time for me to duck out of what was, luckily, only a Med Close Shot. Had it been a Long Shot I would never have made it and so would have been forever visible as a mike shadow on the wall.

I waited until the Guilty Priestess Scene was played again. Oh, joy! My handiwork was visible: the girl was plainly half-nude. Triumph! I have now altered *Siren of Babylon* as well as world history by inserting near-nudity of the topless variety *in a 1948 film*. Done tastefully, as I do everything, I am certain that the scene will be accepted by the Breen Office and the domestic gross of the picture will of course be substantially increased.

I must confess that there is a specific and personal reason for this particular intervention. If the film should become a hit (and I can make it one with a few more alterations), then it will *not* be sold to television in 1950 and if it is not sold to television in 1950 my enemy Mr. Williams will not enter it that year or in any other year, and we shall suddenly find his suite at the Thalberg Hotel empty.

So, baby, the jig is up! You're on your way back to Albany.

Wednesday! In three days I have changed the world. I have made further alterations in the costumes and makeup of *Siren of Babylon*. With extraordinary cunning, I have suggested male and female nudity but in a way that not even the eye of the keenest editor or the most devoted censor could object to: a battle scene in which, for an instant, male buttocks are bared for the first time in glorious color. So quickly does the shot come and go that it is hard to believe one's eyes. Father hills hover in the middle distance while in the farthest reaches of the harem bathing scene there is even beaver. But, as always, Good Taste is my keynote, and of course swiftness. Swiftness is my be-all and end-all.

Each day when I return tired but happy from my labors of creation, I am aware of new tension on the Strip. The telescope in Mr. Williams' window is always turned on me as I come and go from the back lot. Mrs. Connally Yarborough Bowles looks at me with true terror whenever our paths cross and averts her eyes, hurries on.

Maude of course is a comfort. Unfortunately the arrival of Helen Bird has entirely distracted him from our usual diversions. "You don't mind, do you, sweetie? Helen's still a little upset about being here and . . ."

"And you want to know all the latest gossip from Grosse Pointe."

"Not just Grosse Pointe, sugar! Do you know that Helen Bird has given beauty treatments to Rosemary Kanzler in Saint Moritz?"

"And who the burger," I said with some amusement at Maude's impressionability, "is Rosemary Kanzler?"

"Sweetie, really! Your values are so Hollywood and so highbrow."

We had a good laugh over that in the bar of the Mannix. Maude cannot believe that I am not as interested as he is in the doings of the jet set. But despite his silliness, Maude is an invaluable ally and, thanks to Maude's clever fingers and a few beauty hints picked up from Helen Bird, I am now looking like a million dollars, like an absolute dream walking!

Even Telemachus is responding to my seductiveness. He came over to my table after Maude left. "Well, Myron, that's quite a get-up." This oafish effort at sweet-talk misfired.

"Get lost," I jeeped but then had a swift change of mind though not of heart, since I find him physically and morally repulsive. "I was joking." I gave him my Irene Dunne warm little chuckle. Even gave him a touch of *The White Cliffs of Dover*. "Sit down, Telemachus."

Telemachus sat down at the table, eyes staring at me with that awe I am used to no matter how much I may want to be simple, to be warm and immediate, able to forget a happy hour or two my sovereign responsibility to re-create the human race. "Well, Myron, you've been causing quite a stir on the Strip."

"You don't say?" I parried.

"Your ears should be burnt to cinders."

"Oh, dear! My poor rep. That's all a girl has, you know." I was Ann Sothern as the early *Maisie*.

"Yeah. There's a rumor going around that you've been doing things to the flick on the back lot."

I showed him my set of Ann Sothern Disapproving Pursed Lips immediately belied by the Saucy Twinkle in my eyes. "How could teeny-weeny Myra do a thing like that to that great big ole turkey?" Baby talk, courtesy Ginger Rogers.

"By pulling the bras off the chicks and the jocks off the studs." That was brutal.

"You got proof?" Barbara Stanwyck struck.

"I'm just telling you that's the word going around."

"Well, kiddo, I suggest you don't go running off at the mouth if you want to keep that full set of ivories in your fat head."

Telemachus looked alarmed when he saw me reach for my handbag. "Just thought a word to the wise . . ."

"Of course, darling," I husked, having previously shrilled: I like to alternate the two swiftly, for effect. "You don't happen to recall offhand what the domestic gross of *Siren of Babylon* was?"

"One mill two." Telemachus prides himself on knowing every gross by heart.

"Are you sure?"

"Of course I'm sure. Anyway, it's inked right here." He held up the worn copy of domestic and worldwide grosses of all Hollywood products 1930–1968.

I took the book and leafed rapidly to 1948. Eureka! Excelsior! Oh, world! Oh, time! I practically shouted, "It says here one million three."

"I don't believe it. You're looking at the wrong line." He grabbed the book; stared at it; gasped. "But it's not possible."

'*You* must've been looking at the wrong line all along, silly goose!"

I wanted to howl my triumph from the rooftops! But I did not dare, for Mr. Williams may yet try to stop me. After all, once the picture is in the black (and I can put it there in a few more days), no more Mr. Williams on the Strip!

22

When I came to this morning in the cabin of the Mannix, I found out that I have been missing for several days and from the way people act Myra has been busier than a bird dog. Among other things she has destroyed all my clothes so I was forced to dress up in a pair of women's slacks and a blouse but without her goddamn padded bra which I went and shredded the way the big companies and the Federal Government shred their highly secret papers when the Comsymps in the Senate are after them. But more of that anon.

I really believe we are now at the crunch, as in a short while it will be August 1 and we will all be back to square one which is the first day of shooting but I will either be dead by then or out and that's a promise, Myra, you bitch.

Realizing what a funny sight I must look with my short hair and frilly blouse and slacks and wedgies and the awful tweezered eyebrows, I still forced myself to go to the Thalberg Hotel in order to see Mr. Williams and warn him what Myra is up to.

Except for one table of canasta-playing ladies, the lobby was empty, as it was the beginning of lunch in the restaurant. I could hear the out-of-towners in

there yakking away as happy as can be. Only Chicken
was at the desk. He looked shook up when he saw
me and I can only pray that Myra has not tried
anything funny with what is after all a great little
guy.

"What can I do you for . . . sir?" That is a little
joke that is popular with boys that age in California
even now when the moral rot has just begun to set
in of which more anon.

"Is your father here?"

"No, sir. He's gone to Encino to buy meat."

"Well, I want to see Mr. Williams."

"Oh, he's not to be disturbed today."

"Well, you tell him . . ."

Something very strange happened at that moment.
There was like a shadow in the room the way you
suddenly get one in Burbank when a plane flies over
where you are waiting in the parking lot for someone
to land and you're not ready for the shadow to come
because there are no clouds and the smog looks even.

Chicken kept staring at me; his eyes looked really
scared and peculiar and his rosy cheeks didn't look
so rosy but he never took his eyes off mine.

"No, he's not here," he repeated in a hoarse voice.

"But Mr. Williams is always here."

". . . like three months ago." I didn't catch the first
part of what Chicken was saying, as I was talking,
and I didn't know what was three months ago nor
did I care, as I was eager to get to Mr. Williams.

"Well," I said, "tell him that there is a plot against
his life." I thought this would certainly get Mr.
Williams interested in talking to me but Chicken went
right on talking right through me but never taking his
eyes off mine and never losing that really scared
look.

". . . going to be torn down" was all I got out of
what he said after I finished saying what I'd been
saying which he plainly wasn't listening to.

"You sure look good," he said, and then he smiled

and I swear it made me feel real warm all over and wish that Mary-Ann and I could have had a little shaver like Chicken with a Hawaiian shirt and Keds around the house even though we belong to Zero Population Growth and swear by Dr. Paul Ehrlich whose reports on what is happening to the world through overpopulation by the coloreds is just frightening.

"Telephone's ringing," said Chicken, even though I couldn't hear it ringing. "So long now. Have a good day now."

Chicken ran into the office back of the desk and shut the door. The shadow in the room went away, too, and I turned around frustrated as per usual to find Mrs. C. Y. Bowles looking very serious and sad.

At first she was not too friendly until she saw I was Myron. Query: Has everybody here got it worked out that I am sometimes taken over by an enemy or do only Maude and a few others of that ilk understand?

"We have received bad news . . . Myron?"

"Yes, yes, Mrs. Bowles. I'm sorry about this get-up but my clothes are all at the cleaners and I had to borrow these duds from a waitress at the Mannix."

"Say no more." Mrs. C. Y. Bowles showed me a *Los Angeles Times* dated July 19, 1973, which means I have been gone from home for almost four months back there though only a matter of weeks here. "This was brought by a recent arrival. A lady of refinement. From Sherman Oaks. She was studying the listings. For a maid. White. Then she joined our little family."

Well, that paper was full of the most awful thing about what is happening to our President and country that you could imagine. Sometime ago our President bugged his own office so that everything anybody said in it would be all a part of the record and I believe him when he says that he did this so that future generations as yet unborn will have this important historical record of all the important historical things that he and his visitors talked about but naturally the television senators are acting like he did this to get something on the people he talked to who did not know that what they were saying was being recorded for posterity, but as Mrs. C. Y. Bowles said, "Now at last our President will be able to confront his accusers. With tapes of what he *really* said to that terrible Dean Rusk. He will show the world he is innocent."

But I showed her where the paper said that the White House would not let the TV senators hear the tapes.

"Of course they will. In time. First those parts that deal with delicate. And recent negotiations. Between sovereign powers. Intended to ensure peace. With honor. In our time. Will be cut out. In the interest of national security. Then. After that. And only after that. *Altered* tapes will be given to those awful TV senators."

"I hope you're right."

"One ray of light," said Mrs. C. Y. Bowles, "in all this darkness. The Supreme Court. They have outlawed smut. Each community can now decide what it wants to ban."

Well, I was pretty thrilled to learn that the Court says that whatever is obscene is what your average John Q. Citizen thinks is obscene and no Commie talk about freedom of speech and the First Amendment allowed.

23

I lie on the bed of my cabin at the Mannix overwhelmed with grief. During Myron's brief period at the controls this afternoon he learned that in a matter of three weeks we have lost Betty Grable, George Macready, Veronica Lake, Joe E. Brown, Robert Ryan, Lon Chaney, Jr. (the recovery from beriberi was obviously not complete: shall I ring him up to say how sorry I am?) and, most terrible of all, the inimitable, the sublime Ernest Truex so arresting in *The Adventures of Marco Polo* (1938) where his resemblance to the late Harry S Truman gave added resonance to a part that in anyone else's hands might have been secondary. Finally, in this terrible season of falling stars, there died one whom I need not—cannot apostrophize, so close am I to her in every way: Fay Holden—Mom Hardy. If there is a 1974, 1973 will surely be known as Götterdämmerung.

Late at night.

The despair of this afternoon has been replaced by elation. 1973 may yet be a marvelous year. I cannot guarantee that the stars who have twinkled their last twink this (1973) summer will still be alive in the post-Myra 1973 but I do guarantee that they will be working to the end and that the Metro Contract Players system will not be jettisoned and the studio will be in the blackest black. Yes, I have begun my take over of Metro.

I arrived in the bar of the Mannix at sundown, beautifully gowned and coiffed (Myron got off with my padded bra but Maude had an even sexier one in his closet and my bosom now resembles Bonita Granville's in *Now Voyager*). A few out-of-towners greeted me respectfully. Several locals stared with awe and wonder. I radiated charm and quiet authority.

Right on schedule Steve Dude (soon to be Stephanie) entered with a short bald man who wore a large diamond on a finger which he referred to as his "pinkie."

"I see you got my message, Steve." I batted my Miliza Korjus eyelashes at Steve, who blushed.

"I sure did, Myra, and I sure would like to know just how you get these messages to me—I sincerely would, honestly."

I turned to the bald man, who was staring at me with ill-disguised excitement. "You are Mark Dyson." (Steve had promised to bring me the right-hand man of topflight producer Pandro S. Berman).

"No, honey!" How I hated the intimacy in the bald man's voice, the smug male superiority. "I'm Sydney Spaceman. I'm in Casting, and Steve here told me there was this most unusual-type girl holed up at the old Mannix and I told him I'd drop in and take a gander."

"A goose is more like what you'll get."

"Isn't she something, Mr. Spaceman?" Steve is my slave.

"You can say that again."

I was all business. "Do you realize how much money Schary's *Intruder in the Dust* currently being lensed will lose at the box office?"

"A packet, I should guess." Sydney smoked a cigar. Eddie Mannix himself brought us Sazeracs.

"Or the sequel to *Mrs. Miniver* that Sydney Franklin will meg as *The Miniver Story*. Do you know how much that turkey will lose?"

"Lose? It isn't even made."

I had my documents ready. I gave him a sheet of paper with the various pictures currently in production or in pre-production; and the losses (to be fair, I also listed the occasional accident—the flicks that were profitable).

Sydney Spaceman was stunned. "But how do you know all this? How do you know what we're planning to make?"

"Myra's like one of those clear buoyants." Darling Steve is eager to be helpful.

"It doesn't matter how. I know."

Sydney was staring at the sheet, puffing his cigar. I sipped my Sazerac daintily and winked at Steve. Again he blushed.

"How," said Sydney finally, "do you know we're talking about using that whizzer white Garland in a picture which hasn't even got a title yet but you call *Summer Stock*, a lousy title, with Chuck Walters directing?"

"I know, Sydney. I know. And take a look at the red ink. The losses."

To my astonishment and relief, Sydney was able to read the figures I had so neatly printed in red. This is a breakthrough. I had assumed that the ground rules are immutable but obviously they are not. The locals on the Strip cannot read Mr. Telemachus' book of worldwide grosses, yet this very evening top-flight sub-casting director Sydney Spaceman had no difficulty in understanding the report I had prepared on the future of Metro's current product. Obviously the strands of control emanating from Mr. Williams' suite are weakening . . . or there is a way *around* the rules as Mr. Williams was the first to discover some weeks—years—ago when he made his killing on the stock market with future information.

"Now, honey, all this is crazy of course. I mean there's no way of knowing how much a flick will lose *before* you make it otherwise there'd be like no erasers on your pencil." Oh, the smugness! I will break him when I take charge of production. But for now I am playing it warm and womanly, purest Kay Francis.

"Some of us, Sydney, can see the future as it is," I

jilled. "Some of us . . . well, one of us—myself—would like
to see the future as it *ought* to be. That's why I've prepared these figures."

"Yeah, yeah, yeah." *He did listen to Myra Breckinridge.* Before I set down my burden, Sydney Spaceman
will be in the mailroom at the William Morris Agency and
that is a solemn vow.

Nevertheless I continued graciously to jill in my jeep.
"I have my crystal ball, Sydney!" Under the table I
pinched Steve's soon-to-be-detached-from-him bean-bag.
Steve yelped.

Sydney ignored the cry. He was still staring at my report. "What impresses me, Myra," he said at last, "is your
info. How do you know what's being discussed by Mr.
Schary and Mr. Mayer? I'm on the inside and *I* know. But
like take this item for Gable—*Any Number Can Play.*
That's still being scripted."

"Sydney, I know. That's all. Now what I want is a meeting with Dore or L. B. For reasons that are too complicated to go into, I'd like either one—or both—to meet me
here any day this week. They're invited to drop in at the
end of the day for one of Eddie Mannix' special Sazeracs
and a chat about upcoming product."

Sydney gave Steve a look. "You weren't joking."

"No, sir," said Steve. "I wasn't. I sincerely wasn't."

I indicated the various memoranda I have been working
on for the last ten days. "I have a number of projects
that will save the studio."

"Metro is sound as a dollar, honey, and don't need
saving."

I gave him the previous year's losses, this year's
losses and next year's losses but he gave me a superior
smile, an unfair exchange. "O.K. So what're some of your
big ideas? You want us to make you a star?"

"You've done worse." I was cold. "In fact, you've done
no better since Lana was put into orbit. But that is of
peripheral interest. Take a look at Steve."

Sydney looked at Steve, who sat up straight as any vain

young stud will do when he thinks stardom may descend upon him.

"Good-looking kid. He's got a chance on the lot."

"Has it occurred to you, Sydney, that Steve would make a ravishing girl?"

Steve inhaled his Sazerac and started gasping and gagging.

Sydney nearly put his cigar in his mouth wrong way round. "But he's *not* a girl."

"I reckon Myra knows that pretty well." Steve recovered his manly poise.

"Sydney, listen to me closely. This is a biggie. I see this film in which *Steve is turned into a girl before our very eyes*. We'll even show the operation. After all, you can't cheat the audience. Naturally the surgery will be in Good Taste and should occur no later than the second reel. From then on we tell a happy story, the life not of Steve but of Stephanie—a joyous fun-loving sterile Amazon, living a perfect life *without* children, and so an example to the youth of the world, a model for every young male, and our salvation, humanity's as well as Metro's."

For half an hour I acted out the film for their benefit. I confess that I brought tears to my own eyes. When I was finished, there was absolute silence. Steve looked pale and troubled, and Sydney simply looked stupid. "I don't get you, honey. I mean so maybe there's some box office in something so gruesome, like Frankenstein. But what is the lesson for the youth of the world?"

"To reduce world population before it is out-of-hand." I gave them statistics; tried to warn. But as I suspected, the thought is too new in the pre-Myra 1948: the approaching end of the human race is as yet unsuspected.

So I changed my tactic. Tried to show what fun the picture would be. How much money it would make in comparison with, say, *The Miniver Story*. "Here is a treatment I've written—and registered with the Library of Congress, so no burgering around, Sydney. Not that I don't trust you, boychick."

Sydney took the treatment as though he was afraid it

might burn his fingers. "Frankly I can't see L. B. or Dore going for this kind of material. L. B. wants to show wholesome young pig people who love their moms and the flag while doing dumb goyisher things in the suburbs, and Dore likes social uplift."

"L. B. is on the skids with the front office in New York. Dore's on the rise. His success with *Battleground* now in preparation for 1950 release will make it possible for him to do what he wants—for a while, anyway. That's why I'm sure that once Dore knows how important this flick is for all mankind he'll give it the green signal in the name of social uplift."

"How do you know L. B. is on the skids? How do you know *Battleground* is being discussed at the top level?" At that moment I made Sydney Spaceman my slave.

"Darling Sydney, never again ask me *how* I know anything. Just take it for granted that I know it. L. B. will ankle the studio in June 1951."

"What? I didn't hear that?"

For the first time double-talk. I repeated the date. Sydney could not understand me. I wrote the date on a paper napkin. To him it looked like a hieroglyph. Then I led him to the desk of the Mannix Motel and I took down the Utter-McKinley Mortuaries calendar and I flipped to the month of June. Then I pointed to number 1 to 9 to 5 to 1. Sydney understood! Triumph! I have broken the most important ground rule.

"L. B. is leaving June 1951?"

I nodded. I did not add that if my intervention in the affairs of the studio is a success, Schary with his dull uplift pictures will be the one to go and L. B. (shorn of those race horses that ruined his pre-Myra career) will be back at the tiller, making more great product. But I must proceed a step at a time.

"Wow," said Sydney Spaceman.

"Wasn't I right about her." Steve was proud of his creatrix.

"Well, I'm not about to say she really knows future grosses. How could she? But I will say this, Myra, you know everything that's being said out loud in the executive dining room and whispered in the executive sauna."

"So shall we consider my scenario?" I jilled amusingly. "Making *me* into a girl?" Steve was shocked at the idea.

"Well, Steve, you got to admit it's *different* . . ."

"And," I said, "what will ensure worldwide boffo grosses will be that Steve really does become a girl between the first and second reel, and on camera."

"Oh, Jesus H. Christ, Myra! I mean—like keating! I don't go for that. That's crazy." Steve was deeply disturbed.

Sydney laughed. "Well, I don't think we have to go all that far realism-wise. But now you mention it, Steve would be a luscious number with that red hair . . ."

"Oh, come on, Mr. Spaceman, I ain't no fag."

"Nor am I, Steve. But I am like you—a cog in a great industry. You want to be a star, don't you?"

"Well, yeah, but I don't want to lose my powells."

"A small price to pay, darling." I patted his cheek (he shaves, alas, and will need electrolysis).

"We'll fake the operation, if Myra doesn't mind." Sydney seems genuinely intrigued by the overall subject matter.

"You're the boss," I jilled, jeeping to myself. "Until I am."

After a new round of Sazeracs, Steve and Sydney departed. Steve was apologetic. "I got to see my girl tonight. She thinks I been tomcatting too much."

"Don't you want to stay here and let me de-kink you some more, darling?" I was all jill.

"No thank you, ma'am. I'm straightened out for a long time after last time and I mean that sincerely." I did not press the point because I now realize what a coup it will be to transform Steve *during* the picture. Everyone on earth will want to see him before and after. Also, my message to the world will be all the more effective. Close Shot—scalpel. Cut To: bean-bag.

24

I don't know what Myra has been doing but she has been making contact with the locals in a big way.

I got up this morning myself again but shaky and found on the doorstep of the cabin a huge basket of fruit covered with cellophane and silk bows as well as two bottles of champagne and a telegram from someone called Sydney, saying "Welcome aboard," and a lot of other stuff. I suppose she has gone and got herself into the movies which was always her wish. I still have not been able to break her code but it makes no difference now as I have made up my mind that today is pretty near my last day here.

Myra has not found where I keep my clothes and I cannot get at hers without breaking down the closet, so we are even, I suppose. Anyway, I was at least presentable when I met Whittaker Kaiser in the luncheonette of the Mannix for breakfast and there he was with Iris, happy as can be.

"Long time no see," giggled Iris.

"Yeah. Long time." The waitress slapped some coffee down in front of me.

"Oh, he's in one of his moods!" Iris was radiant. "Tell him the good news, Whittaker."

Well, Whittaker was all smiles which is a lot worse, let me tell you, than his usual loony sheriff from Selma, Alabama, number. "We're getting hitched, Myron, I got to have a woman all the time."

"Isn't he cute?" Iris asked me and I couldn't say anything, but knowing what Whittaker feels about the fair sex I couldn't help but imagine her a few weeks from now hanging upside down on a meat hook in the larder after some big quarrel. Of course she is stronger than he is so maybe she can take care of herself. But if I were her I would never turn my back on Whittaker Kaiser.

"Actually she's knocked up, that's why I'm marrying her." There was a lot of cheerful laughter at this and then they talked about all the chidren they were going to have because Whittaker does not believe in contraception.

"How," I said to Whittaker, "can any of us have children back here when we're not allowed to interfere with the locals? And having a child by one of *them* back here is bound to change the future?"

Iris yelled like a wild Indian. "I'm going to find out what that crazy language is if it's the last thing I ever do!"

Whittaker paid no attention to her. "Mr. Williams has given a good ruling. He says that since the baby is never going to get born during our eight-week shooting schedule, there is no serious chance of changing things."

"Yes, but she'll still be pregnant when she goes on into August and we come back to June!"

"Mr. Williams doesn't think so and he ought to know. What really matters is that he's asked Rooster Van Upp to ask me to take over the kitchen of the Thalberg and I've agreed. How could I say no? That's the only game in town food-wise." Then Whittaker went and told us as per usual what a great chef he is and how he would be even better if there was any competition on the Strip or anywhere else for that matter for him to measure himself against, and I left. There is obviously going to be no more talk from him of getting out of here or of kidnapping Mr. Williams. He's settled in. That means I am on my own. The only one who wants out.

I am now back in the movie. That is, I'm at the point where you watch it being made. I am sitting on the ground, my back to that blue-gray barrier I have got to get through *today*. I know the exact spot where our President was shoved through it but for the life of me I can't tell how it's different from any other part of the TV screen.

Technicians walk around me and don't see me. I still find this creepy. From time to time everybody freezes while there is a commercial. Fact, I just now heard this used-car dealer selling his GM lemons on the TV. Also, in the past half hour I have heard several times from behind the barrier someone who I guess is Benjamin R. Laskie the director say, "O.K., action" and "This is a take" and "Print that one."

It is frustrating to know that just behind that glassy whatever-it-is there is a whole real world you can move around in, even if it is 1948.

But there has also got to be another world out there that is home for me because I swear to God that I just now heard Mary-Ann's voice, sounding a million miles away, calling, "Myron, you come up to bed now."

Did I imagine this?

No. She *has* to be there, too, and our TV and rumpus room has to be there with the TV on. Also Pat and Tricia and Julie must also have been there at the White House when our President left them for a much-needed vacation back here unless he was already on vacation with his friend Bebe Rebozo in which case he probably wanted to check out *Siren of Babylon* as a possible emergency White House in case of enemy attack.

Anyway, right after I heard Mary-Ann, I got so depressed and lonesome that I picked up this Babylonian sword that was lying about and started pounding with the hilt on the barrier, but nothing's happened so far and, worse, though I hit it real hard there is no noise either. It is like pounding solid air but I am going to keep at it. Someone will hear. They have to.

25

I have heard, Myron.

We are now at the crunch. The nitty-gritty. Something is about to give. We cannot continue like this: a body divided against itself must decompose, as Raymond Massey might well have said.

I was appalled to find myself hammering at the barrier with the hilt of a Babylonian sword. What if I . . . if Myron had actually broken through to the other side? I shudder at the thought. Even more chilling—he had nearly stepped, by accident, *through the exit*!

Needless to say, I stopped pounding and stuck the sword (which is very sharp) into my . . . Myron's belt. As always, I am excited to be back in the picture. I never tire of Maria and Bruce and Louis—not to mention Steve Dude strutting about in the background, face dark with Max Factor Octoroon.

Myra Breckinridge is still in the picture.

I have been here for two whole showings.

I sit cross-legged now at the edge of the Before the Walls of Babylon Scene, happy to record in this ledger my encounter with J. D. Claypoole, the FBI's principal contribution to Watergate.

During one of the commercial breaks, I walked onto

the set of the Banquet Scene and started to rearrange the Disneyland letters of Jehovah's disagreeable message in order to spell out *my* name on the wall.

I am aware that such a dramatic change in the big sky god's well-known text might smack of self-advertisement, but then, as I am the first to confess, my genius (though universal in its application) is also profoundly American in its nature. Like my countrymen, I am always thrilled when someone entirely without talent is able to become through strenuous and even pathological publicizing of himself a part of the nation's consciousness and for a season famous because that is our American way.

I stress the absence of talent as a *sine qua non* because in a real or even would-be democracy actual excellence is resented and disallowed: witness the constant sniping of the movie reviewers at the truly great films, particularly those starring Lana Turner and William Eythe. What these "critics" do not understand is that the *mythical* aspect of the authentic star made it mandatory for him *not* to act (after all, any idiot can act—look at Laurence Olivier, look at Joseph Wiseman) *but to be*— and need I spell out the simple law that nothing gets in the way of pure being so much as talent (world-making genius of my sort is something else again)?

Take, for example, Ardis Ankerson (known as Brenda Marshall and later of course as Mrs. William Holden) in her first role (*Espionage Agent,* 1939). Ardis demonstrated this mythic quality in spades. With her high cheekbones, sharp chin and bright hazel eyes, brunette Brenda-Ardis radiated godhood—another Pallas Athena in the line of Frances Farmer. *But Ardis did not receive the support that she deserved from either the press or the Industry.* Also, she was too shy to draw attention to herself—and why should she? Is the Virgin Mary expected to hang out a sign in front of her bungalow? or buy space in the trade papers when Oscar-time comes around? So Brenda-Ardis and Bill Holden were married and she retired from the silver screen and I only hope, *pray,* that she has found some happiness in her private life—a long shot, I fear, since Holden as star is no more than pale carbon to a true mythic figure like James Craig.

"What the burger are you doing, Breckinridge?" was Claypoole's greeting to me as I tried to substitute the second letter of Jehovah's message with a "Y" (the first letter, significantly, is "M").

"Out of the sight line, you FBI fruit!" I shouted as I hurled the letter "Y" at his head and it connected. Unfortunately it was made of plastic (the letter "Y"—not the head, which is of solid bone) and hardly creased his crew-cut.

At that moment we were pulled out of the set and the action began again. I was thrilled to see that Jehovah's message on the wall lacked an "e." I hope there was consternation in the Valley at this lacuna but I doubt it, since reading skills are agreeably low in Southern California.

"You know the rules, Breckinridge. Jesus! Look what you've done to the writing on the wall! Typical Commie trick. Don't think I don't know what you're doing: sending your messages to your Chinese friends, the way you do in those fortune cookies. Don't think I haven't got your number, Mac, because I have." This confused harangue was heard by me with a small patient Eve Arden smile.

"Are you on duty here?" My voice was plangent only a hint of jeep.

"*Special* duty, Mac, assigned by Mr. Williams himself. Mayday. Mayday." Claypoole was sweating and for all his bravado I detected terror in his dull eyes. But then, who does not fear his creatrix?

"I must be about my work, keating-head." I smiled at him as I started to turn away.

"No more interfering. That's an order."

I responded to this "order" with three or four peals of Deanna Durbin girlish laughter.

Claypoole then pulled a revolver from the holster under his jacket. Luckily for me, in the grand old lavender-and-lace tradition of the FBI, the revolver was backwards in its holster. For an instant Claypoole held the weapon by its muzzle. As he started to switch it around, I let him have the Archangel-Three-Wing-Twist and Chop.

The gun flew in one direction. Claypoole flew in another. With a grunt he reeled backward *into the action of the picture*, and what I have from the beginning suspected was an axiom of this not only parallel but uniquely vertical universe proved to be true: Claypoole's momentum was so great that the delicate rejecting force that keeps us out of the action was not able to expel him; instead, he entered the scene and fell into the open arms of one of the officers standing just behind Nebuchadnezzar's throne in the Council Scene. The extra seemed not to notice what had happened, since we are no more than mike shadows to players who are to us divine images on celluloid.

The scene continued without a hitch, but my original theory about this special universe (whose laws I make and so must joyously obey) was perfectly demonstrated, for like two bits of mercury pushed too close together, the actor absorbed Claypoole. For an instant I saw two men, one clinging to the other. Then there was only one: the extra. If I were interested in Claypoole's fate, I would take the time to work out *where* he has gone (if anywhere) but I have other tasks to perform prior to tomorrow's meeting with Dore Schary. In fact, time is of the essence if I am to halt nature's planned death for the human race in the late (pre-Myra) seventies.

I removed from my pocket the dental floss that Myron always carries about with him. I tested the Babylonian sword on the floss. The sword is sharp as a razor. Obviously some extra has been playing around with the props.

At the start of the Battle Beneath the Walls of Babylon Scene, the longest of the commercial breaks begins. The soldiers freeze. From behind the blue-gray barrier I could hear the far-off voice of a used-car salesman.

I ran to the nearest soldier, a burly young man who

stood with legs wide-spread, spear in hand, looking up at the painted canvas walls of Babylon.

I pulled up the military skirt and tucked it under his belt. He wore no underwear. A nondescript American rosebud stared at me with its blind eye looking somewhat startled, if such lethal objects (capable of filling up the universe with hungry replicas) can be said to have expression. The powells hung loose in a crinkly scrotum.

Deftly I took the sharp point of the sword and made an incision in the man's right groin. I know by heart where all the tubes and arteries are hidden. With hindsight, as they say in Washington, I confess now that I was fearful that there might be bleeding which could not be stanched since I had no clamps, but to my relief, the blood was as frozen in the young man's veins as everything else. He could not bleed any more than he could move or breathe during the commercial break when all the players are in a state of suspended animation like so many live frogs congealed for the winter in a pond.

With the dental floss I quickly tied off the seminal tubes. Then I repeated the same operation in his left groin. A perfect vasectomy! And far better than surgery in a doctor's office because not a drop of blood appeared on the pink skin.

When the tugging began, I had just time enough to pull down the soldier's skirt.

I hurried across the sight line as the commercial ended and the action began.

I was on tenterhooks! Would he notice what had happened?

Bruce Cabot's magnificent voice resounded across the desert. "Charge, oh, men of Babylon!"

My soldier (my creation!) had been frozen with his spear aimed at the walls of Babylon. As the action started, he suddenly dropped the spear and grabbed at his crotch as though someone had kicked him. For an instant the soldier clutched at himself. Then, very stiffly, he started to walk out of frame. The battle continued, as always.

I was waiting for him—not that he could see or hear me. I stood next to a technical director who spends most of his time going back and forth through the barrier with instructions from the director.

"What's wrong Sam?" The technical director actually knows all the extras by name, but then, Metro is one wonderful family under the benign fathership of Dream Merchant L. B. Mayers, whose bacon I mean to save.

"I think I got hit with a rock or something." I looked at the man's heavy-set bare legs, fearing to see blood trickling down. But my sutures held.

"Go see the doc."

"Yeah." The extra walked shakily into the blue-gray barrier. I was relieved. He will now get proper medical attention, and best of all, he will never be able to add another human being to this pullulating planet.

An hour after my successful vasectomy of a member in good standing of the Screen Extras Guild, Mr. Williams himself appeared on the set. He wore a panama hat, a white suit, carried a cane—very natty all in all, and very frightened.

"You must leave the film immediately, Mr. Breckinridge. That is an order."

"How can what *I* have invented order me to do what I have no intention of doing?" I felt the power rise in me. At last we were face to face, Myra the creatrix and the uppity dinge from Albany, New York.

"The question of *a priori* invention has no single and certainly no satisfactory answer."

"You see the answer all about you. You see it in my eyes, don't you, Mr. Williams? You see the end of the game I allowed you to play for twenty-three years. Now it's over. I am about to put this picture *in the black*."

"That is not possible. The past is past. What was is."

"What is *was*, Mr. Williams." Like a gladiator in the divine *Quo Vadis*, I swung the enmeshing net of my dialectic over Mr. Williams; then hurled at him the trident of my logic.

"I am here as the savior not only of Metro-Goldwyn-Mayer but of the human race."

"No, you are simply here to meddle. To be absurd. To change for your own amusement the balance of history."

"You prefer that I let the studio make *The Miniver Story*, and lose a packet? Do you prefer that a quarter century from now the nearly doubled population of the earth will suffer from famine, from lack of energy, from the collapse of Western civilization as represented by the as yet unmade films of Bertolucci and the dread Peckinpah? Do you prefer that I allow one billion too many people to be born when I—and I alone—can stop their conception right here at the source? Finally, do you in your heart of hearts really want to see Kerkorian and Aubrey at the helm of MGM?"

Mr. Williams was staggered by the Greek fire of my argument. But he did his best to rally. "You cannot change anything that is essential. Even if you could, you must not because this atrocious studio—this dispenser of slick kitsch—must die. The cinema, the most depressing and demoralizing of all pseudo-art forms must be destroyed."

At last the horrible, the unsuspected, plot was revealed. I was, I confess, staggered and sickened.

Like the total villain, the world-destroying monster he is, Mr. Williams did not spare me the full horror of what he has done. "Yes, Breckinridge, I am destroying the cinema, bit by bit, step by step. Why do you think *The Miniver Story* is being made? And all those other turkeys? Because *I* have got through to the front office! It is *my* advice they are taking, not yours!" Oh, the enemy is more cunning than I suspected. I am still shaken by this exchange.

"The Word must regain its primacy—which is what is happening now. As of 1973 worldwide box-office grosses have plummeted—thanks to what I am doing here—and the crack in the golden bowl is once again visible to the young people of the seventies who laugh at Lana Turner as they read Holkien and Tesse and Vonchon and Pyne-gut."

I could not let him rave on. As I have suspected for some time, Hollywood has been controlled for twenty-three years by a demented educated Negro: an erratic black comet loose in the Gutenberg galaxy just as that galaxy spirals into extinction to be replaced by the electronic picture which flashes classic films from television set to television set, from eye to eye, all 'round the world, joyously bouncing off satellites as it unifies in beautiful simultaneity a world for centuries kept in solipsistic disarray and separation by the written and the (invariably) wrong word.

"I see your grand design, Mr. Williams, and I am happy to be able to shatter it. You are my creation."

"No! No, Breckinridge. You are my aberration."

"This is my universe."

"It is mine. Look! Darkness. My darkness." Mr. Williams pointed at the dark sky opposite, to the inside of the TV set where we are lodged.

I laughed at him like Bette Davis in *The Little Foxes*. "Shall I give you proof of my power? Shall I send you back to Albany in 1950? There to die in due course, long before 1973?"

"You cannot." But I saw the terror in his black face.

"I can and I will. I shall put *Siren of Babylon* in the black."

"You don't dare!"

I raised high my Babylonian sword. "In the first reel, with a single gesture, I shall change the history of the cinema, and send *you* back to Albany."

With a horrendous cry, Mr. Williams *fled*. There is no other word; if there was I would not use it.

I sit now writing in this book, waiting for the picture to begin.

My plan is simple. Just before Maria Montez enters the set for her first scene, I shall unsnap her breastplates.

From Encino to Van Nuys the audience will be ravished. More to the point, I am certain that that scene will be accepted by the Breen Office in (pre-Myra) 1948 because . . .

The *CREDITS* are starting. The MGM lion just roared.

Here comes Maria Montez. She has just left her trailer on the other side of the barrier. The makeup man is with her. How beautiful she is!

26

I am Maria Montez.

27

For eight glorious days I have been—and am—Maria
Montez, the star of stars at Universal Pictures currently
on loan-out to MGM for *Siren of Babylon,* in a deal
pacted by top-flight ten-percenter Louis Schurr.

It is Sunday. I sit at my beautiful writing desk in my
palatial home at the corner of Tower Road and San
Ysidro. Through the windows I can see my Japanese
gardener pruning my roses. A tourist bus has just gone
by, and I could hear the guide saying, "That's the house
where Maria Montez lives with her husband Jean-Pierre
Aumont, the French film star."

Jean-Pierre. *My* husband. My magnificent eyes brim
with happy tears as I think of him, of our happiness
together. Of our darling daughter Tina, aged two years
old (she was born on St. Valentine's day 1946)—and taking a nap as I write these lines.

At times I find it hard to remember that I am still
Myra Breckinridge, on temporary duty, as it were, within
this gorgeous body so soon to die.

I look at myself in the mirror on the wall opposite. I
am . . . *she* is so beautiful! I *must* find some way of preserving her—of preserving us. I have already told my
darling Jean-Pierre that if ever I say that I am going to
Arden's to lose weight in the hot paraffin baths, he is to

stop me. But Jean-Pierre just laughs. Apparently Maria Montez is just like me: a willful spitfire—yet fun-loving, gracious, womanly, a star!

I have Mr. Williams to thank for this exquisite experience. In a desperate attempt to save himself, he vaulted me from dull earth to radiant paradise.

As Maria Montez stood, waiting for the cue to begin the first scene of the picture (though not the first scene to be shot), I started toward her, ready to tastefully adjust her costume.

When I was a few feet from Maria Montez, Luke suddenly appeared: a mountain of a man, who is—was—from foothills to peak devoted to Mr. Williams.

"Get lost, buster!" I jeeped.

Luke lowered his head, and like a maddened buffalo, charged me.

I immediately struck the Early September Gourd position, but for once I fear that I was too slow: the mountain was moving faster than Mohammed realized.

Luke knocked the wind from me—something no man has ever done before or ever will again. That is a vow.

Clutching this ledger in one hand, I fell backwards against Maria Montez (needless to say, none of the people on the set were aware of Luke and me).

It is a most peculiar and disagreeable sensation to collide with a body that simply does not respond. Maria Montez did not feel me hit her. I, on the other hand, felt it jammed into my *poitrine,* not to mention the barbaric spikiness of her right earring as my face grazed her cheek.

Then darkness: a sense of being sucked into a vacuum. For an instant—an eternity?—I did not exist. There was nothing. Time stopped. The universe vanished as its creatrix ceased to exert control over her gorgeous finitude of starry spirals.

Finally my eyes opened of their own accord and I saw a different world from any that I have ever seen before.

The sky was an intense cobalt-blue; brighter than any sky could ever be this side of Natalie Kalmus and the

Technicolor process. Yet it was no more than an authentic 1948 California sky seen with 1948 Santo Domingan eyes.

From far away I heard the makeup man say, "A little powder, Miss Montez. We're getting a shine."

I looked about me to see where I was and discovered that I was where I had been before. Only everything was now different. That was my first reaction and, as always, it was precise, despite obvious disorientation.

Right off, I knew that I was not myself—or rather, that I was myself but someone else as well. Myself *augmented* by someone marvelous rather than *diminished* by something cretinous like Myron.

Next I realized that all my senses are now different from what they were. The sky to my new eyes is more vivid than any I have ever seen before outside a movie. My sense of smell is more acute—no, not more acute, different: I am conscious that I move in a cloud of gardenia scent that protects me from the slight sweet sweaty smell of the makeup man who is applying powder to my forehead. I shrink from the odor, not liking it (because I do not like him?). I also hear in a new way. The sound of grips laughing and joking in the distance annoys me; makes it hard for me to concentrate, and concentrate I *must* in order to achieve absolute mental clarity, for I am the star of the picture and, presently, will be obliged to climb a steep wooden staircase at the back of the "marble" staircase down which I shall soon, superbly, descend.

Looking back, I still turn to ice with a terror that is remembered not in tranquillity but in glory.

I am standing there. I am nervous. I am breathing hard. I am perspiring beneath the golden breastplate.

The makeup man knows that I am jittery. He murmurs soothingly, "That's fine, Miss Montez. And those new eyelashes are real beautiful. You look like a million."

"Thanks," I say. *My voice is different!* No longer do I possess the fabulous range of Myra Breckinridge, who could, at will, re-create a dozen stars with no more than a sigh or a gurgle of laughter. No, the voice now is bronze. The voice is a trumpet. The voice is that of Maria Montez.

I am she, I say to myself, and she is . . . me? I start to shudder convulsively. A sudden panic. Will I be able to give a performance? Can I, very simply, cut the mustard?

"What's the matter, Miss Montez?" It is the assistant director.

"Nothing." The voice—the marvelous voice—is coming from me! "I think I'm a little faint. The heat."

In an instant a folding chair with *Maria Montez* painted on the back is brought me. Then the director hurries over to me. Benjamin R. Laskie himself (one of the metaphysical arguments on the Strip is now answered: there *is* a Mr. Laskie, and a camera crew, and a camera, and a studio beyond that). The blue-gray barrier no longer exists for me: I have made the journey to the other side traveling, need I add, first class.

Laskie is short, fat, with a nose like the bowl of the pipe he always holds clenched between his yellow teeth. "Hey, baby doll, you under the weather?"

"On top of it, Mr. Laskie." I flash a smile at him and would have given a fortune to be able myself to see and enjoy the smile that clearly rocks him, as it does all normal men.

"*Mr.* Laskie! How about that! Well, baby doll, you're the boss. When you want to roll, we roll."

As much as I enjoy the badinage between superstar and staff director, I *am* nervous. Although I have seen *Siren of Babylon* perhaps a thousand times and know all the dialogue, I am fearful that I might not (oh, shame to confess even to this ledger such weakness, such uncharacteristic timidity!) that I might not be able to play what, after all, is one of the most difficult roles ever essayed by any star of the silver age.

I also realize the terrible responsibility that has suddenly been thrust upon me. History requires me to give a performance which will not be topped (at least pre-Myra) until Lana's luminous work in *The Prodigal*, almost a decade later.

"I'm ready." I pull myself together, conscious of my beauty, of my total command.

"You got all the words, baby doll? You want I should get you your coach?"

Coach? What could he mean? Dialogue director, I assume. Or perhaps Maria is studying English, since her accent is quite pronounced. Curious. Although I am a master of the English language and think entirely in English, whenever I speak, Maria's accent takes control. A lucky thing for our career, but puzzling.

Slowly I climb the steep staircase in back of the set. I am conscious of the sharp smell of raw pine and I am careful not to let my skirt sweep against the occasional viscous splotches of oozing resin. If there is one thing a star hates more than a tropism, is's a viscosity.

At the top of the staircase I stop and wait for my cue.

Ecstasy. No other word. I, Maria Montez, the most beautiful woman on earth superbly if barbarically gowned and exquisitely coiffed, am standing on top of a flight of shallow simulated marble stairs.

Lights on huge cranes are focused on *me*. A mike boom is above my head. Beneath me stands Louis Calhern, as Nebuchadnezzar, waiting for me to descend, fearful of my oracle.

Beyond the set I can see past the back lot to the gleaming white sound stages of Metro—until now hidden from me by the blue-gray barrier.

I look in the opposite direction, toward the Strip, where I can see the crummy Thalberg Hotel, not to mention the unspeakably sordid Mannix Motel; and I wonder how I had ever settled for such a sleazy life. I, who was born to be a superstar in my native Santo Domingo, I mean Red Bank, New Jersey.

Does Mr. Williams suspect what has happened? Are the out-of-towners watching me? But of course they are. Myron has just arrived. He and Maude are standing at the bottom of the stairs. I narrow my eyes: yes, there are two unaccountable shadows just below me. Then the lights are readjusted and the shadows of Maude and Myron vanish.

Laskie waves to me. "O.K., baby doll. We're rolling."

I hear the bronze trumpet of my voice say the dialogue I have heard a thousand times but never dreamed that I myself would one day say not only for the camera but for all time, "Greetings, oh, King of Babylon. From the goddess whose servant I am!"

I cannot believe it is I. The grips as well as the extras are transfixed with delight and awe as I begin my descent, every inch of me a goddess. Even Louis Calhern, a supercilious New York stage star, cannot keep out of his face an expression that can only be described as worshipful.

"I come with gifts, oh, Priestess, for the Sun." Mr. Calhern comes in late on his cue, as usual, and I (always a good sport) have to return to my place when Laskie yells, "Cut!"

Mr. Calhern says, "Oh, damn. Sorry, Miss Montez. I was off my mark."

"It could happen to anyone," I say graciously, always the star and yet warm and human with everyone, even featured players from the New York stage who look down on Hollywood and only come out here to make money. Well, *we* know camera, and camera is the only thing worth knowing.

The day of triumph ends when I throw my arms up to heaven and pray to the Goddess of the Sun to defeat the enemies of Babylon. So powerful is my reading of this very beautiful speech written especially for me at Dore Schary's insistence by Leonard Spigelgass that the grips burst into spontaneous applause when I finish and Laskie shouts, "Print it!"

On a cloud called Nine (an expression one often hears in 1948 though what its origin I know not), I am borne to my trailer (exquisitely frilly and pink), where makeup is removed with the help of a maid and I put on my usual clothes, a glamorous star-style Travis Banton creation with open-toed shoes.

I allow the maid to arrange my hair, since I have not a clue as to how Maria Montez looked off-duty circa 1948. Now I know: *on duty*. To be a star is to be constant, immutable, shining.

A chauffeur-driven limousine whisks me through Culver City—how empty the streets are compared to now (1973 pre-Myra) with half as many cars, I should think.

I stare through the car window like a Martianess, delighting in the quaint costumes, in the crewcut boys—until I realize that my glances might be misinterpreted and I must not, in any way, compromise Maria Montez, a Universal superstar and sex symbol who is, nevertheless, a *perfect* wife and loyal in every way to Gallic heartthrob Jean-Pierre Aumont.

My darling Jean-Pierre. What happiness I have known this last week! Except for one thing. I cannot understand one goddamned word he says because he insists on speaking French to me, the son of a bitch, and when I say, "No, no, my dearest. Let us practice on our English like my coach says we must," he just laughs and jabbers away like a deranged wine steward.

It is a great strain, which I am beginning to show. Not only does he keep talking French to me but the only people we ever see in this town are *not* Lana, Judy, Bette and Dolores Moran, who are at their zenith, but all the goddamned French actors like Charles Boyer, who is, I must confess, a treat to look at even without his hairpiece but *what* the hell is he talking about all the time, what are *any* of them talking about?"

"Caramba!" I exploded last night after dinner here at home with a dozen French-talking Europeans mostly under contract to Warner's. I do intersperse my conversation with Spanish words and phrases picked up from the PRs who used to hang around Columbia when I was Myron the First and a fixture in a local bar frequented by youths of the lowest class.

"We must practice our English, *muchachos*."

But it did no good. Everyone laughed and this French or German writer whose name I still don't know (and obviously I don't dare ask him his name since Maria Montez is an old friend of his and a lapse of memory of that sort might have serious repercussions), this writer with the face of a lion and the brain of a burnt-out orangutan did his party number which consists of gulping down the contents of a huge glass of brandy and then chewing up the glass (in our house Baccarat crystal) and swallowing it. Everyone is thrilled when he does this except me. I hope he hemorrhages internally.

Last night when he finished munching on the crystal, I shouted, *"Ole!"* Then I threw open the door to the cabinet where our beautiful crystal goblets are kept, and said, "Start eating, *zapata!*"

The roar of laughter from the guests was reassuring. I am obviously convincing in the role of a fun-loving superstar but I have been, I must confess, deflected these last few days from my true goal, which is the salvation of MGM in particular, and of the world in general. The two are interrelated, as I mean to prove.

My position now as Maria Montez is not the bowl of cherries it might seem to the casual observer. Although I am in a place of power, I am far too conspicuous to be able to operate freely. I must watch not only the usual p's but the troubling q's. I am also seriously handicapped by being unable to use Maria Montez's memory. There it all is, in her head, completely available to me except for the fact that all her memories are in Spanish, and since I have not the time to take a crash course at Berlitz in order to rob the memory bank, I am obliged every minute of the day to "wing" it, as we stars say.

28

Back on the set of *Siren of Babylon.*

I am giving the performance of the decade. Everyone says so. The daily rushes are studied by L. B. and Dore, and Laskie says, "Baby doll, the studio's yours! Nobody but *nobody* dreamed you could give a performance like this in what is—let's face it—a corn you cope ee ah."

"Caramba," I said, smiling brilliantly. "Each flick we make during this period can be only one thing, immortal— you dumb kike bastard," I added, throwing in a half dozen Puerto Rican gay chuckles.

"You break me up!" Laskie gasped, breaking up.

I firmly believe that I am now able, *through perform- ance alone*, to put *Siren of Babylon* in the black, eliminat- ing Mr. Williams, whose diabolic advice to the front office here has until now been creating turkeys galore.

Once Mr. Williams is safely back in Albany, I shall have a free hand to create a new product. To introduce a cycle of Beat films. To revive the Andy Hardy series (I saw Mickey, the adorable little shaver, in the commis- sary yesterday and he *whistled* when he saw me!). Fi- nally, I must put a stop to *The Miniver Story*. I also ex- pect to get—no, I must be fair—I expect Maria Montez to get the Academy Award for the performance I have been giving on the back lot during these last ten days of shooting which include all the key character scenes.

An amusing encounter in the commissary at lunch today. I entered the noisy room with top-flight ten-percenter agent Bert Allenberg—a tall, ugly, amusing man who wants to get me away from Louis Schurr, but I am totally loyal. Nevertheless, I enjoy Bert and we are the best of friends.

Just inside the commissary door, before you get to the writers' table on the left where Leonard Spigelgass reigns supreme, I ran into Sydney Spaceman and Steve Dude. Steve gasped, the way extras do whenever they come face to face with a total star.

"Steve!" I flashed my full smile.

"Gee, Miss Montez. You remember my name!"

"I make it a point to know the names of all my fellow workers in this great Industry."

"I'll go get us a table," said Bert, who only handles top-flight six-figures talent and plainly did not want to be bothered with an extra like Steve or a sub-casting director like Sydney Spaceman, who said, eagerly, nose-browning, "The rushes are just great, Miss Montez!"

"Thank you." I was mischievous. "I hope you are making plans for that big picture, starring Mr. Dude?"

"What was that again, Miss Montez?" S. Spaceman could not believe his ears.

"The world is waiting to see—*Stefanie*! The first fun-loving Amazon, to be created especially for the screen."

"Jesus H. Christ!" Steve Dude was stunned.

"How did you know about that—uh, project, Miss Montez?" S. Spaceman was bewildered.

"Because I do not make a movie without consulting Myra Breckinridge. All us stars do. She is, frankly, infallible. I must confess to you that, believe it or not, I was dubious about the script of *Cobra Woman*. Quality-wise I feared that it lacked class. Well, Myra convinced me that I could overcome the dialogue and I did, as the world knows! *Caramba*!"

Bert came back. "Table's ready, Maria."

"Where is Miss Breckinridge?" asked S. Spaceman. "I made an appointment for her with Eddie Mannix here a few days ago but they said she wasn't living at the motel any more."

"*Quién sabe?* Myra travels far and she travels fast. But do exactly what she tells you to do, Mr. Spaceman, and you will triumph." I blinked my dreamy dark eyes at Steve. "Stefanie," I whispered. "You will be a star. You will change the world. Obey Myra." Their minds are blown.

I enjoy lunching in the commissary and always refuse to take a star's table, preferring potluck. I also enjoy passing between tables crowded with extras and featured players wearing colorful costumes. On all sides I feel their worship, and draw strength from the ecstasy they feel in the presence of a superstar on loan-out from Universal.

I am always stopped at least half a dozen times by people who know Maria Montez or pretend to know her. I am gracious—and at least they all speak English, unlike that floating crap game of French-talking lounge lizards at home. I must have it out with Jean-Pierre. It'll do his career no harm to practice his English with me.

Bert was most interesting at lunch. "You're wrong, you know, about wanting to change your image."

"But I don't want to change. What gave you that idea?"

"You did. Couple weeks ago. When I saw you at Joe Pasternak's house. You said you wanted to give up the sex-symbol business. Underplay the father hills. Be like Paulette Goddard, who you said gets away with murder and doesn't have to throw her whizzer white around on the screen."

I smiled. "I am a big tease, dear Bert." I really laid on the PR accent. "I love Paulette and respect this girl's taste in jewels but I am happy like this. The way the good God made me." I threw out my *poitrine* and cried, "*Ole!*" to the merriment of those nearby.

Then after we had our laugh Bert got down to business and told me top-flight producer Sam Zimbalist of *Boom*

Town fame is considering me for a project and would like to meet me. I graciously agreed to an appointment.

I also learned to my amazement that I am—that Maria Montez is—on the skids at Universal and that she has been inked to topline a little stinker in France next month with Jean-Pierre and Lilli Palmer. I must nip this project in the bud. For one thing, Maria Montez must make a major Hollywood film next. For another, how the burger am I supposed to make a flick in French when the only sentence I have picked up so far is *Je m'en foute?*

29

I seem to be gaining a little weight and must watch the old calories. Fortunately, I know a great deal about dieting, a subject no one understands back here. They think that if you want to lose weight you must sweat, which is idiotic and dangerous, as poor Maria Montez will soon demonstrate unless I find a way of saving her.

I am tempted to become a beauty counselor. With what I know about the emetic properties of grapefruit, I could make a fortune.

Tomorrow is the last day of shooting. There will be a party on the back lot. Will the shadows of Mr. Williams *et çie* be on hand? But I forget. Tomorrow is August the first, which means that they will all be heading back to June the first, thank God.

After today's shooting I went straight to Mr. Zimbalist's office and we had a most interesting and fruitful conversation. I truly believe that I have now begun the salvation of Metro.

As I swept imperiously into the inner office, Mr. Zimbalist came from behind his desk to greet me. He is tall, with a loud deep voice. Although he has the blue lips of a carp, his eyes have a warm twinkle and he is a genuinely good person as well as a top-flight producer with a track record that is the envy of all Hollywood despite the shellacking he is going to take on the upcoming *Beau Brummell* unless I intervene.

"Miss Montez! I'm glad you could take the time to come see me."

"Call me Maria . . . Sam!" I husked in a PR way, and then sat down on the legendary director Sydney Franklin, whose presence in the room I had not noticed since he is very small and gray and had not risen to his feet at my entrance; he had remained seated as "I am not feeling so good, Miss Montez. Please forgive me."

I forgave him. He forgave me for sitting on him. I noticed with surprise that he was wearing gloves. Later Sam told me that Sydney was afraid of germs!

I took the bull by the horns, as is my wont. "Sydney, do not—I repeat—do not make *The Miniver Story*. You will lose a packet for the studio and seriously affect your own track record as a bankable staff-megger."

Sydney and Sam were stunned that I knew so much about a project still under wraps. "Nice meeting you, Miss Montez," said Sydney, creeping to the door. "I'll bear that in mind what you said about *The Miniver Story* I really will."

"Let's hope he does, Sam." I flashed my teeth at Sam Zimbalist. Pushed out my *poitrine*. Tossed my head so that the earrings jingled (holes have been pierced in my ear lobes—I confess that it took me an hour to get up sufficient nerve to put on my earrings for the first time).

"Maria, I've got a couple of properties that might interest you. We're all pretty impressed by the work you're doing for Ben Laskie. The dailies all last week were sensational and everybody's talking about them in the executive dining room. I give away no secrets when I tell you that L. B.'s kicking himself that Universal got you instead of Metro."

I accepted this flattery as my due. It is true that Maria Montez's performance in *Siren of Babylon* was marvelous (pre-Myra) but she lacked the *total* authority I have brought to the role. After all, Maria Montez never saw herself play the part a thousand times. I have. I also know how to gild your average lily.

Laskie is stunned that I now do every scene in a single take. "Baby doll, you got perfect concentration. I don't know what's come over you the last few days."

Sam chuckled suddenly. "Laskie's being a naughty boy. Some of the stuff he's trying to get away with! L. B. was fit to be tied when he saw that scene where the girl has no top to her costume.

"Did L. B. *cut* the scene?"

"Of course. You can't release a picture with a scene like that. Funny thing is, Laskie swears it was an accident. Some joker, that boy! But if the picture is profitable that's all that counts."

Not until I see the final edited version of the picture will I be able to determine to what extent my changes have remained in the film. It is a fact that the last time I looked at Mr. Telemachus' domestic grosses I had added a hundred thousand dollars to the total. Was this increment a result of the performance I am now giving or of earlier changes? It is all very puzzling. Obviously I must put time in its place. If I don't, that tragic pre-Myra world of Nixon, Peckinpah and Paul Morrissey will so derange the world's monetary system that the making of multinational picture productions will be a financial no-no.

I enjoy Sam. He worships me. I can tell. But we are decorous. Each happily married. Fulfilled. He has a wen on the back of his neck.

I warned him about *Beau Brummell*.

"How did you know we were thinking along those lines?"

"Because I do and because I care and because I love this Industry. Sam, I'll tell you what I want to play. *Ben-Hur*. As a silent, Metro made a packet on that flick first time around. Now *you* make it again as a talky, as a *super* spectacular!"

Sam narrowed then popped his eyes at me: a trick many people back here do in imitation of top-flight megger Vic Fleming, a he-man who is everyone's idol except mine. "Funny you should mention *Ben-Hur*. Dore and I were talking about the property at lunch today."

"Don't just *talk*, Sam. Make the picture! Make it *now* for release in the early fifties—not the late fifties." I was tactful. Did not tell him that he would indeed produce *Ben-Hur* in 1958, and during the production die in Rome of a heart attack brought on by the harassment from a panicky post-Dore Schary front office complicated by a lifelong habit of each day drinking several quarts of milk and cream. Sam's *Ben-Hur* is his monument, of course, and it did save Metro briefly. But my plan is more basic. If the picture were to be made in 1948 instead of 1958, Metro will be able to weather the fifties and L. B. will be at the helm until his pre-Myra death in 1957.

"That's not much of a part for you, the girl friend of Ben-Hur," said Sam.

"*Caramba, Samba!* I mean Sam." We both broke up at my funny error. "I want to play the part of Ben-Hur."

"How?" Sam looked stunned.

"The way I am playing the *Siren of Babylon*, the way I play everything—like Maria Montez, superstar."

"Well, this is an unusual approach, Maria, and I'd better sleep on it. Off the top of my head, I can't see L. B. going along but . . ."

"Good taste will win the day, as it always does with me. I won't play Ben as a man and I won't play him as a woman. I will play Ben-Hur like Montez, larger than life!"

"I see what you mean," he said, seeing.

I think I have half convinced him. But he did not react as well to my idea of transforming Steve Dude into a fun-loving sterile Amazon. Sam did think, however, that if there was sufficient uplift in the presentation, Dore might be willing to try it on for size with the leadership of B'nai B'rith and Planned Parenthood.

All in all a successful meeting.

As I was coming out of the Thalberg Building, where my car was waiting beneath the magnolia tree, I saw

Judy Garland talking to top-flight musical-comedy producer Arthur Freed. They were talking very earnestly to
each other and she was clutching at his arm, and frowning. It was strange, suddenly, seeing Judy, who has been
dead for four years now (1973), still alive and pretty if
a bit plump and troubled.

I came up behind them, not knowing if she was a friend
of Maria Montez or not. "Judy!" I said, projecting superbly.

Judy Garland jumped like a frightened gazelle. "Maria
Montez! Oh, God!" Judy started to giggle uncontrollably.

"Ole," I said firmly, pushing Arthur Freed to one side.
"I want to say a few words to you, Judy. In private.
Because no one else has the courage to tell you."

Still giggling mysteriously, hysterically, Judy accompa-
nied me to the foot of the magnolia tree. I saw in the distance a half dozen fans approaching down the street,
coming from the funeral parlor which shares the site of
the executive building. We would only have a minute together.

"Judy, you are destroying yourself with drugs and
booze."

That stopped the giggles. "What do you mean drugs?"
There is—was—an Irish spitfire in Judy. Unfortunately,
she had no neck; otherwise, she was every inch a star.

"Nembutals are barbiturates and barbiturates are
drugs like heroin. You're about to miss the chance of
your career with *Annie Get Your Gun*."

"I'm making it. And what the burger business is it of
yours . . ."

"You're going to be replaced by Betty Hutton."

"You've got to be kidding! Betty Hutton makes Deanna
Durbin with that penguin arm look talented." Here Judy,
I fear, did a cruel imitation of her rival girl singer and
fellow immortal Deanna Durbin, now happily retired to
France.

The fans started to shout our names.

"Cut the clowning, Judy. Put yourself away. Dry out.

Get off the pills. If you don't you'll be dead in twenty-one years."

"That's a hell of a long time off and besides . . ."

The fans were upon us. Regally signing autographs, I made my way to the car. I shall save Judy yet.

I told my chauffeur to go home by way of the Strip. Morbidly, I wanted a last glimpse of the out-of-towners before they go back to the first day of shooting tomorrow.

"Stop here," I said as we approached the Mannix Motel.

If memory serves, I am on schedule, I thought as I got out of the car. It was dusk and though several locals saw me as they entered the bar, I was not recognized.

Just inside the bar Maude was sitting with Helen Bird, drinking daiquiris. Maude gasped when he saw me. I held my finger to my lips and flashed an intimate glance at him. I was so placed beside the jukebox that the other inmates of the bar could not see me clearly.

Maude hurried over. "Miss Montez, this is an honor! I'm Nemo Trojan but call me . . ."

"Maude. I know."

"You do!" Maude was delirious with joy. "May I have the honor—the *privilege*—of planning a totally new coiffure for you?"

"It's too late, I'm afraid."

"Too late?"

"Because you go back to the first day of shooting tomorrow and I shall go on into August." I must say it was wicked of me to stun poor Maude like that but I could not resist a little mischief.

Maude's round damp face was a study in putty. "You *know?*" he hissed.

"Everything."

"How?"

"Myra told me."

"Where is she?" There was now real terror in Maude's face.

"Off the Strip."

"I know. I heard. But *where?*"

"Safe and around. She is my constant adviser. Tell Mr. Williams that, thanks to Myra, I am certain to get the Academy Award for my performance in *our* movie!"

"Oh, no! Please, Miss Montez! Stop her! Stop Myra! This picture has got to bomb or we're all done for."

"Only the early arrivals like Mr. Williams will be done for. Don't worry, sweetie. The picture will have been sold to television by the time you hit the Strip."

"But it won't be the same!"

"Nothing will ever be the same, thanks to Myra Breckinridge."

"Maria Montez!" I heard a familiar voice behind me. I turned and there was Whittaker Kaiser in cook's apron and chef's hat. He was now impersonating a serious earnest breathy criminal of the Nixon variety. "I've always had this existential idea of you, Miss Montez. I've always felt that what you needed was someone like me, not only a real man in a feminized world but a cook who understands not just the black beans and rice you were brought up on but the castrator goddess you represent, despite your vulnerability."

"Why don't you"—and margarine would not have uncongealed its vegetable fats in my beautiful mouth—"go burger yourself? You dumb . . ." I sought a Maria Montez word. Found it. *"¡Cucaracha!"* I even remembered to pronounce the exclamation mark upside down in the Spanish manner as I swept out of the bar and into my limousine, confident that I had now totally demoralized Mr. Williams and sent him back to Albany.

30

It is late at night in my beautiful mansion on Tower Road. Jean-Pierre is sleeping. Crickets can be heard in the garden. A lovely silvery moon casts shadows through my window. The air is scented with jasmine. I am perfectly happy but deeply troubled.

We must not make that film in France. But Maria Montez has signed the contract and Louis Schurr says we must go through with it. I don't know what to do.

Sam Zimbalist is eating out of my hand. He is activating the *Ben-Hur* property. At Warner's, Irving Rapper is willing, he tells me, to show on the screen the transformation of Steve Dude *if* I agree to play the part of the plastic surgeon. Although I am too big a star for what is only a supporting role, I told Mr. Rapper that in the interest of curbing world population I would even consent to do a cameo, so strongly do I feel on the subject. Finally, Sydney Franklin has decided not to go ahead with *The Miniver Story*.

All these marvelous things are beginning to happen, thanks to my being so well located in time and space. But now we must go to France where that blackmun writer is waiting for us to buy him some more brandy glasses to munch on. I am in despair.

Yet I must count my blessings, too. It is wonderful being Maria Montez, even if I don't understand a word my darling Jean-Pierre says to me.

Where, I sometimes wonder, is Maria Montez now that I am where I am? Is she deep down inside? If so, will she ever forgive me for having put two pounds on her magnificent body in the last few weeks? I have, by the way, gone to the doctor. Maria's heart is sound—so it is simply bad luck what is going to happen three years from now when she takes that hot paraffin bath at Arden's. A terrifying thought: if she dies, will I die? Is this possible? Although death is simply Mother Nature's way of saying slow down, am I pushing too hard? I must try not to brood. *Che sarà sarà*. And I have my work to do.

Busy days now. Making plans. Packing. Studying French in secret. Soon I'll be *acting* in French. *Zut alors!*

Tomorrow I make a personal appearance at the opening of a branch of Penney's in downtown Los Angeles. Curious the sense of *déjà vu* I have—as though I have done all this before. Yet of course I have not. This is the first time. It has to be.

My darling Jean-Pierre. I have just kissed him on the forehead. He is smiling in his sleep. Does he dream of me? How happy we are.

31

I don't guess I'll ever be able to make any sense out of this ledger which has gone with me through thick and thin. So much of it is written in a funny kind of code which I have so far not been able to crack and so I will probably never figure out what Myra was up to but I can guess—*no good!*

I was able to read the part where she is or thinks she is Maria Montez and it is funny now that I think of it that this part must be true because I now remember everything about that morning when my mother Gertrude the practical nurse happened to read in the paper that Maria Montez would make a personal appearance at the opening of a branch of Penney's in downtown L.A. where we had been visiting my uncle Buck Loner, the Singin' Shootin' Cowboy Star of Radio and so on.

I can still hear Gertrude saying, "I got to see that swell-elegant Maria Montez in the flesh and I'm taking Myron with me even if the doctor does say he should be kept in a strait jacket all the time."

That part—the out-of-my-head part—I don't remember at all as I was off my rocker for about three weeks. But I sort of remember hearing in my head Gertrude discussing going to see Maria Montez.

Then next thing I know there is this crowd in front of Penney's with newsreel cameras, and all of us fans lined up on the sidewalk, waiting until this limousine drives up and out steps Maria Montez, looking very tall and beautiful though, frankly, after my experiences inside *Siren of Babylon,* I am not very eager to see her ever again or any other movie star for that matter on the TV or anywhere else.

Well, as the flash bulbs go off and the newsreel camera buzzes away, Maria Montez makes her way through the crowd. When she gets to us, my mother Gertrude the practical nurse says, "Oh, what a thrill it is, Maria, meeting you who I have always thought the absolute tops!" Or something like that.

As Gertrude says this, I can still remember after what is now one fourth of a century the way Maria Montez's eyes suddenly open wide and her mouth just falls open. She starts to back away from us but Gertrude has grabbed her arm.

"I want you to meet my little boy Myron who loves all your movies, though he has not been himself lately, jabbering away in this language nobody can understand though of course he can talk as plain as you when he wants to but he won't talk at all now. He just sulks all day."

While Gertrude the practical nurse is saying all this, Maria Montez just stares at me, her face white as a sheet. Then she gives a funny little cry, "Oh, no. No!" There is pleading in her voice.

So that was it. The crunch. The next thing I know I am sitting here in the TV and rumpus room in front of the TV, watching the last credits of *Siren of Babylon.*

I think I have got a pretty good idea now of what happened. As Myra wrote, she became Maria Montez and Miss Montez became me—but me as I was back in 1948 aged ten years old. I can imagine what a shock it must've been for your average world-famed movie star like Maria Montez to have to spend three weeks of her valuable time inside yours truly aged ten years old. What she was talking all that time through me that nobody could understand, thank God, was her native Spanish. Then I guess once she figured out that she was stuck and that complaining would do no good, she just clammed up and hoped for the best which finally happened in front of Penney's that morning with me.

Of course, Maria Montez then went right on the way she was meant to go on and in due course she took that hot paraffin bath at Arden's and conked out, I'm sorry to say. But the moving finger, once it has writ, moves on and there are no erasers, Myra to the contrary—thinking she could change the world, given enough time back in 1948 and an expensive wardrobe.

Much relieved to be home again, I went straight upstairs and crawled into bed beside Mary-Ann who was sound asleep.

32

We are having a barbecue in half an hour and I am filling up the last pages on this ledger while the coals are burning in the barbecue pit out there in the back yard.

I have been deeply troubled as are we all by the Constitutional crisis of today, Sunday, July 29, 1973. The TV senators are demanding the tapes that the President has made of his many historical conversations in his various offices around the land. Worse, however, is the request of his own son-in-law Cox for copies of those tapes, even though Cox works for the President, too.

Fortunately, Mr. Nixon is going to hang tough and in this frame of time he's going to hack it, I am sure, although many of his admirers in the Valley are upset as who is not?

A funny thing happened this morning. I drove over to Culver City to a butcher I know who sells dandy sirloin for a barbecue and after I bought the steak at the price so ruinously high that you can well believe that the Communists are deliberately wrecking our economy by buying up all the grain so that the cows and baby chicks have to be killed because the cost of feeding them is too high for a profit thus making shortages galore in the richest and best country on earth, I decided it might be fun to see if the Thalberg Hotel is still standing so I drove along the Strip where I spent so many awful days and nights.

Well, you wouldn't recognize anything. The movie house where *Call Northside 777* was is gone as is the Mannix Motel and everything else except for, believe it or not, the Thalberg Hotel which is still there, very run-down as it is about to be torn down.

I parked in front and went inside the lobby which is very different than it used to be, modernized with lots of neon but dusty and likewise run-down.

There was no one in the lobby but behind the desk was this fat baldheaded man who was just staring into space, talking to himself.

Fat and bald though he was, I recognized Chicken Van Upp. "Hi, Chicken," I said, "remember me?"

Well, he looked scared to death and started mumbling how the hotel was no longer in business and being torn down.

"Where's Rooster?" I asked. "In the office?"

"No, he's not here."

"You've put on a little weight, Chicken."

"Fact, he died like three months ago."

"Sorry to hear that, Chicken," I said. "What're you going to do with the hotel?"

"It's sold. Going to be torn down."

"Sorry about that."

"You sure look good," he said. Well, there wasn't really much more we could say to each other after that. Then the telephone rang. "Telephone's ringing," said Chicken. "So long now. Have a good day now."

As I turned around to go out, I thought I saw a card table with four ladies sitting at it playing canasta. But that was twenty-five years ago and when I blinked my eyes this sort of double-exposure effect went away.

I felt kind of sorry to see how Chicken has aged

and also sorry that there isn't much point for us to go fishing together or skinny-dipping as he is now older than I am and because he's fat looks even older than he is which must be forty-one or two.

Well, I am nearly at the end of this ledger. Everything has turned out all right for yours truly and after the latest series of hormone injections I don't think we'll ever be hearing from Myra again.

I am also happy and relieved that nothing serious was dislocated by all the crazy things she was allegedly up to back in 1948 on the Strip. It's the same old country that is was when I got into the picture with a lot of problems, true, but also with the know-how how to solve those problems in the good old American way like John Wayne tells us on the new disk he has just cut.

One peculiar thing just cropped up that did make me a little uneasy. Last night when I was calling up different people to invite them to today's barbecue, I called Sam Westcott who is a very able attorney in Van Nuys and active in Republican politics. "Sam," I said, "you old galoot, why don't you and Becky come on over for some barbecue like around sundown tomorrow?"

"Sure would feature it, Myron." We talk Western together, our joke, you might say.

"And bring the young genius."

"The young what?"

"Bring Sam Junior if he's around so as we can congratulate him on getting that Nobel Prize."

There was this silence on the other end of the line. Then Sam said, "Myron, are you plumb loco? There ain't no Sam Junior. You know I been a stud mule since before I married Becky and used to hang around all them starlets when I was doing extra work in the movies and had one of the first spontaneous vasectomies ever recorded by medical science."

"Hell, Sam I was just joshing you," I said and

quickly told him the latest joke about these two Mexicans. Sam likes Mexican jokes.

But it is real strange that Sam Junior doesn't exist now when I know for a fact that he was the fair-haired boy of the whole country before I got into *Siren of Babylon* with his population-control efforts which were all the rage with whole countries asking him to come on down and help them out.

Well, maybe I imagined all that about Sam having had a son, just like I allowed the out-of-towners to convince me that *Siren of Babylon* had been a flop in its day when of course it was a smash hit and Maria Montez was awarded the Academy Award for her performance.

Thank God, Myra was not able to change anything at all except maybe keeping Sam Junior from being born, and despite her meddling, this country is just like it was which is just about perfect no matter what the Com-symp senator from Massachusetts John F. Kennedy says as he starts his race for the President by unfairly and maliciously taking advantage of Mr. Nixon's current misfortunes.

Luckily, there's not a chance on earth of John Q. Citizen buying Mr. Kennedy's radical line since his only claim to fame is being the brother-in-law of Marilyn Monroe which is hardly sufficient qualification for being the President of these United States, as our good governor and next Republican President Stefanie Dude, the fun-loving Amazon, said last night on the television during an interview from the governor's mansion at Sacramento.

Since there are only a few blank lines left to this page, I will sign off by saying that the highly articulately silent majority to which I am darned proud to belong are happy with things as they are and that we are not going to let anybody, repeat *anybody,* change things from what they are.

33

Isevil aryM

About the Author

GORE VIDAL wrote his first novel at nineteen while overseas during the Second World War. *Williwaw* (1946) is still regarded as one of the best American war novels. In the forties Vidal was known chiefly for *The City and the Pillar* (1948), the first American novel to deal openly with homosexuality.

In the early fifties, Vidal wrote two of his most distinguished novels: *The Judgment of Paris* and the prophetic *Messiah*. He also wrote a number of plays for live television (1954–1956); one became the Broadway success *Visit to a Small Planet*. Directly for the theater (and later for the screen) he wrote the prize-winning play *The Best Man*.

In 1964, Vidal returned to the novel. In succession, he created four remarkable works: *Julian* (1964); *Washington, D.C.* (1967); *Myra Breckinridge* (1968); *Burr* (1973). Each became the number-one best seller not only in the United States but in England.

Other recent works are *An Evening with Richard Nixon* and *Homage to Daniel Shays,* a collection of his essays from 1952 to 1972.